THE BUTTERFLY EFFECT

EILIS O'SHEA

ISBN: 9798554507199 (Paperback)

ISBN: 9798554507199 (Ebook)

Any references to historical events, real people, or real places are used fictitiously. Names, characters, and places are products of the author's imagination.

Book design by Eilis O'Shea.

Printed by Amazon, in the United Kingdom.

First printing edition 2020.

www.eilisoshea.com

For my friends and family
Who were the beginning of my very
own butterfly effect

The Butterfly Effect:

noun

(in chaos theory) the phenomenon whereby a minute localized change in a complex system can have large effects elsewhere.

PROLOGUE

Alice

ALICE was late. That being said, Alice was always late. But Alice was particularly late because on this occasion when she had left her Aunt's lavish city penthouse. She had not anticipated that what would ensue was a series of never-ending stops and starts in a queue of traffic that seemed to never make any distance.

It might have been because Alice had been in a hurry that morning or perhaps because unusually Alice's mind was not consumed by something other than concentrating on where she was going but whilst this meant a despairingly long and arduous journey to NYU's campus. It did also allow for more of the world to actually be taken in than when Alice was in her normal state of mindful disarray. She had noticed small little interactions between passers-by. A quaint little café tucked away on a street corner she passed every day but had never been "with it" enough to fully recognise. People sat outside in the last of the summer's sunshine with various beverages and plates of food. Sitting on small tables in front of them. Some doing work, others reading books. Some were just watching the world go by.

Alice wondered if this was what she looked like when she was in her normal state of mind. It was most likely both away with the fairies and up in the clouds at the same time but did *she* look as if she was actually very present to the world. As if she was paying very close attention to each and every detail in front of her. Or, more likely, if she resembled a somewhat half transformed zombie more than a socially conscientious individual.

It was at this point, however, that she realised she had returned to said normal state of mind by which time she had now reached the roadside of Washington Square Park. She couldn't have travelled more than a mile since her last conscious thought.

Groaning, Alice leant forwards to lean her forehead against her steering wheel. After moving to America had wiped out hers and a large majority of her parents' bank accounts it was a very pleasant surprise when Alice's glamorous and very, *very* American aunt had gifted her with the brand-new MINI Cooper upon her arrival. Alice had been immensely grateful, of course, but while Alice may well spend ninety percent of her time locked inside her mind either over-thinking or avoiding thinking about anything at all. One might consider Alice to be an excellent judge of character.

Alice's Aunt Isabella was her Mother's half-sister. Born in her father's second marriage to an American charity worker *coincidently* working in the Middle East the same time her father was on a "business trip" in the same place, Isabella had spent her entire life grappling for attention from anyone she could grab hold of and wrap round her little finger. A trait virtually encouraged by her oh-so-glamourous job writing a column centred solely around who was dating who in the media. Alice herself had only met her Aunt once before when she had married her equally American and prosperous husband.

At the time, most of the family had secretly hoped it would quench her thirst for attention for a couple of years. For every ounce of thirst for attention that was quenched, however, double the amount of inclination to show off her new wealth replaced it. This mainly consisted of lavish gifts and tremendously over the top favours so when Alice and her parents politely refused her offer to pay for Alice's tuition fees at NYU or even travelling expenses it wasn't too hard to deduce that the car was a way to keep Isabella in the thick of it all. So, Alice accepted it graciously (and, admittedly, rather excitedly).

Nonetheless, Alice was very aware of how lucky she was to have Isabella in her corner. While her incessant gifting and "beneficial" interference with almost every aspect of Alice's new student life in New York made her feel uncomfortably indebted. Alice was in no position to decline free accommodation. Especially when it was as luxurious as it was and the car would have been almost as essential to her as the penthouse if it weren't for the horrendous New York traffic.

Turning her head to peer into the grassy area of the park beside her, Alice pondered if she really had been better off getting the subway like she had considered before leaving when her train of thought was cut off abruptly by a flash of yellow catching her eye. Curiosity perking her up, Alice lifted her head once again to get a better view of the scene to see a large grassy area of the park closed off by bright yellow police tape.

In it, various official looking people of differing ranks and departments swarmed the cut off zone. As some carried out their respective tasks, others stood in close huddles of important looking people talking secretively, glancing every now and then at a large white tent constructed almost dead centre of the sector. Intrigued, Alice craned her neck as if she may be able to see into the enigmatic and somewhat hurried erection only to sit back against her car seat hastily when, unexpectedly, an NYPD cap covered head entered her line of sight as a young looking officer strode up to her driver's side window.

Alice let out a sigh of relief as the officer rapped on the glass of her window lightly signalling her to open it. The shock of his unexpected arrival has sent her, once again, preoccupied mind into a flurry of momentary panic but quickly, Alice composed herself as best as she could and plastered a friendly smile on her face, habitually pushing her wireframe glasses further up the bridge of her nose.

The age old glasses she had, had since childhood were a little too big for her now after her face had slimmed down from her chubbier prepubescent days. She, like many others, carried a little bit of puppy fat but for years now they had been slipping down the bridge of her nose whenever she had worn them but she was in such a hurry that morning that locating a pair of much more practical contact lenses had been forced right to the bottom of her priorities list. As a result, Alice had settled for the much more easily acquired glasses she normally reserved for longs days at home as she had rushed out of the door. She now realised, however, that the resultant struggle to keep them on as she awkwardly opened her window compliantly almost wasn't worth it. Smiling kindly the officer leant forwards to rest his elbows against the window looking laid back and somewhat casual. At least it wasn't *her* who was in trouble.

"I'm sorry about this, Miss" The officer spoke, his bold and unmistakable New York accent filling the car "But we're having to divert all traffic down to third street for the time being while we get this mess cleared up" Quickly Alice nodded starting to put her car into a gear. "Of course," She replied eager to move on with her journey and away from the officer.

It wasn't that she herself had something to hide exactly. It was that Alice had always found herself acting ten times more suspicious than was socially acceptable when in the vicinity of a police officer. There was something about their judgmental gazes and almost unconditional authority over another person that made you feel you *ought* to be hiding something or another at any given encounter. Generally speaking, Alice was a very empathetic person, but police officers were one type of person Alice just couldn't find it in her to relate to. The sooner her interaction was over, the better.

 "You headed to the university?" The officer questioned, astutely observing Alice's casual NYU sweatshirt as she prepared to turn into the now moving traffic being guided by another slightly older officer. "Um…" Alice hummed temporarily preoccupied with stopping her car before turning back to the officer and taking a second to recall what he had asked. "Oh!" She let out the question now fully processing without the distraction of keeping a car stationary. "Oh, y-yeah" She stammered, glancing almost longingly at the line of traffic moving in the lane beside her. "I-I'm late for my lecture" She explained, hoping that her discreet excuse to get away would speed up the process of ending the conversation a little.

 This was one thing Alice could do without. Back in London no one had time to chat but here in New York it was almost like an obligation to ask how someone's day had been. It had been the start of many unwanted and forced conversations Alice had been subject to. The inclination to make small talk wasn't at all in her British conditioning unless absolutely necessary and on this occasion. It most *certainly* was not necessary.

Thankfully though, the message was received and almost immediately the officer removed his elbows from her window and touched his cap politely. "I won't keep you then, miss" He answered nodding his head as he began to make his way to the car behind her "Have a great day" He called after her as he turned to face his direction of travel and Alice hurriedly pulled out of her lane into the line of traffic moving towards third street but not before risking one last glance at the scene causing all this commotion.

All the way down third street towards NYU Alice reverted back to her normal introverted state of mind as questions rattled in her head with no apparent answers. What was the haphazard white tent concealing? Why did it require such a large amount of people to clear away? And more importantly, why did it mean the entire area had to be closed off?

PART ONE

CHAPTER ONE

Mark

MARK wasn't always late. Just most of the time. Then again, Mark was in an occupation in which people practically expected one to be late. Tradesmen had never been known for their punctuality least of all the young ones but that didn't stop him from arriving on time every once in a while, just to see how the next clueless middle-class homemaker would react.

There *was* one, however, that Mark didn't mind arriving on time to, or sometimes even *early,* whenever he received a call from the softly spoken housewife of a busy New York banker. Admittedly it was selfish motivation. Mark enjoyed the motherly fawning he received anytime he spent any given amount of time in the distinctive American family household and the keen interest her only son had in whatever it was he was doing. Marjory was one of the few people Mark had worked for that could make "a semi decent cup of tea" for want of a better phrase and her homely suburban house almost always smelt brilliantly of some baked good, cooked just that morning (of which Mark was always entitled to his fair share).

Mark would be the first to admit he enjoyed the blatant adoration he received in said household. Phrases like "Oh you clever boy!" and "Wow, that's wicked!" thrown in the air by both their mother and the children fuelled Marks egotism enough to last him to the next call he would receive from them (there was always a next call). Unfortunately, though, the call he was responding to today was about as far away from his favourite household as was humanly possible.

Currently, he was stood in front of a front door, badly screwed to the worn doorframe surrounding it, that had been painted a disgusting colour between khaki and luminescent snot in a dank and damp ridden corridor. Sighing resentfully, he raised his free hand once again to knock on the door for what felt like the hundredth time when suddenly the door opened as far as the chain behind it would allow, revealing the face of a greasy, bloated man behind the safety of the slab of wood. Momentarily Mark grimaced as the stench of beer and old Indian take away attacked his sense of smell and made his eyes water before gulping down his disgust and repeating the phrase he had formulated long ago that explained his appearance on a strangers doorstep in as little amount of words as possible.

"Someone call about a broken boiler?"

Wordlessly the man closed the door again before a scratching of metal against metal could be heard and the door was reopened, fully this time.

"This way" He grumbled, waving Mark in begrudgingly. Mark raised an eyebrow. He had half a mind to turn and leave the building altogether if this man had started as he meant go on. Mark was aware that he wasn't exactly a life-saving doctor, but he did know that he most certainly deserved more than a grumble and a somewhat irritated sideways glance, as if he had inconvenienced the man greatly, by way of thanks. Nevertheless, he stepped into the second-rate city flat of the grouchy man and followed him through a small, untidy living area, decorated only by cheap IKEA furniture covered in various coffee stains and marks of dirt, into an even smaller kitchen.

The room, if it can be called that considering there wasn't a whole lot of "room" provided, was dinky and unhygienic. The counter tops were covered in dirty tin trays of differing take-aways and new layers of limescale were accumulating over those already existing on a suspiciously neglected looking kitchen sink, piled high with dirty dishes. Again, Mark scrunched his nose up at the state the man was living in.

Mark didn't pretend to be some big shot businessman by any stretch of the imagination. His own flat can't have been much larger than the one he was stood in right now but at least he didn't live in a tip. Granted, his belongings were few in numbers and his decoration stretched only to a semi-forgotten painting acquired (by means he now no longer remembered) in his short lived college days but he still took pride in the care of those few possessions despite no one ever baring witness to it. He himself spent very little time in the feeble home he had somehow pulled together with the few possessions he owned after he had dropped out of college.

Frankly, it was a miracle he had anything at all after his shock decision to pull out of the prestigious engineering course he had begun at NYU two years previously following a series of equally jarring events leading up to it. His father had stopped working long before then after his health had declined rapidly and any money left of the little savings he had built up after moving to America from Taiwan with nothing more than a suitcase and his four year old son went towards medical bills and any basic living expenses. It left Mark with no other option than to pay his own way through life.

There were times when Mark had wondered if maybe it was that god damned diagnosis that had started all the complications in his life. Like that theory where one flap of a butterfly wing can cause tsunamis in places miles away.

Maybe that diagnosis had been the pebble that had been dropped in the serene pond of Marks quiet, relatively unextraordinary life. Maybe that had caused the series of one giant wave after another to knock poor, young, naive Mark against the rocks of the big wide world over and over again. Maybe if his father hadn't become so ill, he might have taken better care of himself at that time. Instead of working two part time jobs just to cover the cost of his tuition fees and spending the little time he had outside of working, getting drunk by himself on the deserted rooftop of the subpar building he resided in then latterly with the sort of people that made you wish you were alone. Maybe if the night his father crashed suddenly, he wasn't doing just that, Jacob wouldn't have had to drop him off at the hospital because he was too off his face to drive and maybe… Maybe he would still be here.

Blinking suddenly Mark jolted back to present time when he realised the man had finally stopped talking and was now looking at him expectantly for an answer to a question Mark had inevitably missed. Quickly Mark glanced down at the now exposed boiler in the corner of the room. It didn't take long for him to figure out what was going on once his eyes had glanced over the pressure gauge. Low pressure was one of the most common problems with boilers these days but what was causing it was another question.

"Um…" Mark drew out moving towards the gurgling machine before setting his toolbox down beside him as he lowered himself down to one knee in an attempt to see under the large appliance. "It depends" He spoke making an educated guess that the question the man had asked would have something to do with how long he was going to be in the way. "If it's a leak" He explained reaching underneath the boiler to check the pipes for any water dribbling down them. Soon enough Mark's hand came into contact with warm liquid trickling down one of the long copper pipes leading up to the boiler from the ground. Just his luck.

Letting out a long breath through his nose as he pulled back to kneel back on his feet and rest his hands on his thighs. Mark could already feel a headache coming on from the way it looked the day was going and the lingering nausea from last night's binge on alcohol didn't help his sleep deprived state either. He knew he should have just risked being even later and stopped for coffee before he came to his first job. It would have saved him a whole lot of exhaustion, but he had soldiered on all for some grumpy pervert.

"An hour… Maybe two"

CHAPTER TWO

Alice

IT was at around lunchtime that Alice started questioning her life's choices and it was approximately five minutes after that, that Alice came to the realisation that it wasn't her lack of motivation that was the cause but rather her lack of coffee. Her *liquid* motivation. Like "liquid luck" but more... student-y. Alice had never really needed the aforementioned "liquid luck" when taking into consideration the fact that she had never felt so inclined to do something so outrageous that "liquid luck" was required. She was, however, very familiar with her own variation of the concoction.

Though she much preferred a cup of tea over the bitter taste of a cup of coffee she very quickly realised, during her many hours of exam preparation before moving to America, that tea, unfortunately, didn't have quite the same energising effect as the latter option. Many a night of studying had been driven by an endless supply of the drug like beverage and once she was through the last set of her national exams, she had found herself somewhat addicted to the drink. Something that was only encouraged upon her arrival in the states.

So, realising that anymore time spent in the stuffy library of NYU would be time wasted unless she got some coffee into her system, Alice packed away her books and pens and automatically headed towards the coffee shop over the road from the study area. It had been the only coffee place Alice had been to in the entire city since moving which, given the fact that it was in America, was quite the feat. Not once had it ever let her down - with the exception of a subpar cup of tea she had once ordered but no one there was pretending to know how to make a cup of tea.

"They really ought to know how to make a cup of tea, though" Alice had mumbled as she had immediately thrown it away in the nearest bin that was out of the eyeline of any barista in the coffeeshop. Granted, it was called a *coffee* shop but doesn't that, generally speaking, rather suggest that they offer a slightly wider collection of hot drinks than *just* coffee? Like… Hot chocolate? *And* tea? This one even offered soft drinks and yet they wouldn't know a proper cup of tea unless it fell into the teacup in front of them, having just spilt a glass of one of those putrid ice teas Americans love so much.

That was another American thing that baffled Alice. Why would someone take a perfectly decent cup of *hot* tea and then decide to let it go *cold*? The thought process was beyond her but still, despite the undeniable reliability of her usual coffee shop when concerning the very drink Alice wanted, today she hesitated. Quietly she weighed up her options as the small café she had passed earlier that day crossed her mind reminding her once again that *her* coffee shop wasn't the *only* coffee shop in the big city she now lived in.

Alice had been meaning to try to widen her berth of the famous New York City for a long time now but no matter how hard she worked, it seemed for every assignment she managed to complete, three more would be thrown at her. She had done well today, however, and today Alice had been very productive, whatever was left she could do in a coffeeshop quite easily.

Before she realised what was happening consciously, Alice was already moving towards her MINI parked on the side of the road outside the library when suddenly an irrational fear that one of the baristas in *her* coffee shop may spot her, gripped her chest. It wasn't actually a *fear* as such. More of a feeling of social obligation.

Alice had once felt the same way when she and her parents had opted for a fish and chips takeaway over a curry one Friday night. Unfortunately, both their local chippy and curry house were located on the same road, almost directly beside each other and as they entered the fish and chips place Alice had found herself feeling unreasonably guilty. Like she had betrayed the trust of the friendly restaurant manager, Jay, in the neighbouring Indian place and had found herself trying to speed the entire process up to avoid getting caught in the act. Much to the confusion of her parents.

Just like then, Alice was quick about yanking the car door open and throwing her work carelessly across the gear stick to sit on the passenger side seat as she climbed in almost as chaotically as her papers had entered the small car and certainly as awkwardly. Clumsily, Alice fumbled with her car keys dropping them twice into her lap as she struggled to find the right key to slide into the ignition before, third time lucky, she dropped them right over the gap between the driver's and passenger seats.

Irked at her failed escapade, Alice huffed, blowing stray strands of hair from her face as she took a moment to collect her thoughts. There was no way anyone can have seen her in that shamble so that was that problem fixed but now she had a new problem.

In the form of an MIA keyring.

Except it wasn't really MIA because she knew exactly where it was. It was how to get it she didn't know.

CHAPTER THREE

Mark

WHEN Mark was finally happy that the boiler he had been working on for the last hour and a half wasn't going to start leaking again anytime soon, he allowed himself a sigh of relief. Under normal circumstances he might have left it long ago and let it start leaking just to give him some work later on but decidedly this was *not* a place he wanted to revisit. Investing a little more time today was definitely worth it if it meant no more would be required further down the line. It did mean he required at least two cups of coffee right now, at this point in time, to get him through the rest of the day at least *half* alive.

The question was. Could he wait to get to a place that didn't look *painfully* American or was he desperate enough to settle for the overpriced chain coffee shop he was parked opposite? For a moment, Mark seriously considered the potential of the large shop strategically placed opposite the NYU Bobst Library waiting to lure in naive students thirsty for their next caffeine hit but quickly he shook the thought, reminding himself that not ten minutes away was a much cheaper, much better shop when suddenly there was a dull thump from beside him.

Surprised, Mark moved his gaze away from where his second-hand Vauxhall Corsa was parked to look down at the cream MINI Cooper parked beside him as he passed, curiously looking for the source of the noise. Unmoving, the car let out an irritated and pained groan as Mark peered in through the windshield to see a dishevelled looking student rubbing the back of her head as she pushed a pair of too big wireframe glasses further up the bridge of her nose. Looking suitably peeved she huffed slouching back against the driver's seat with her arms crossed over her chest and a small, slightly morbid part of Mark found the charade almost amusing.

Unbeknownst to the poor girl, Mark chuckled as he walked straight past, still none the wiser as to what had irritated the girl so, but his day was looking slightly less dull than before as he came to a stop beside his own car. Placing his toolbox down beside him, Mark pulled his car keys from the deep pocket on the side of his tradesman trousers but before he had a chance to unlock the vehicle his attention was once again shifted to the MINI as the driver's side door was opened and the student climbed out of it.

The girl was dressed in casual black jeans and a grey NYU sweatshirt with a pair of newer looking VANS trainers. Her long somewhat tangled hair fell over her face as she clambered out clumsily, causing her to blow it disdainfully as she straightened up before tugging on the hem of her sweatshirt and turning to look down the street both ways as she once again pushed her glasses back into place.

Mark was taken aback when she swivelled to face him a half exasperated, half desperate expression on her face causing her softly shaped brows to pull together to create a more of an 's' shape. The girl was neither astonishingly beautiful nor notably *un*-beautiful. In fact, impossible though it seemed, she appeared to be both *and* neither at the same time. Like someone had taken very *ordinary* body parts and put them together to create one quite extraordinary whole being. Apart from her eyes. Her eyes were anything *but* ordinary.

It was hard to see with the sunlight glinting off the lenses of her ridiculously large glasses but hidden underneath the glare was a pair of alarmingly bright blue eyes that seemed so out of place on the petite somewhat monochromatic girl. With her pasty white complexion and bland light brown hair colour, they seemed to belong to someone else entirely. And yet Mark found them intriguingly, striking. Like a pop of red lipstick in an other wise black and white photograph or flash of light glinting off a diamond in an other wise darkened cave. It caught him so off guard that Mark found himself frozen with his keys half raised for a moment as he took the girl in fully before he realised that the girl's lips were moving as she faced him also.

"P-pardon?" He stammered lowering his hand to hang at his side uselessly. "I said, do you think you can help me?" she repeated leaning against the still open door with her elbow closest to it "I've dropped my keys down the gap of the seats" she explained tugging her hair behind her ear even more irritably.

Mark took a moment to think. He had a magnet in his toolbox just beside him but the effectiveness of that idea depended on the type of metal the girls keys were made of and if it was the wrong type of metal then he had a hook but *that* method was significantly more time consuming. Mark was already desperate enough for a cup of coffee without the added delay of helping modern day damsels in distress in the middle of fourth street but was there a socially acceptable way for him to *not* give her the help she needed? Then again… Had there been a time when Mark Liu cared about the social consequences of his actions in the last year and a half?

"Sorry" He answered as casually as he could lifting his own keys again and unlocking his Corsa "I'm running late for my next job but if you can find a magnet or a hook then that's your best bet" he advised, as if the meagre counsel would compensate for the obvious ditching he was giving her. Quickly the girl frowned looking put down as Mark opened the door of his car when suddenly the girl's expression changed. Slowly a smile grew on her face before a chuckle fell from her lips and another, until she was almost bent over double with uncontrollable laughter.

Baffled Mark hesitated to slide into the Corsa as he watched the girl in confusion. Most people would be pretty peeved that he had just left them stranded but this girl looked positively overjoyed at his cold action. The humour of the girl laughing so inappropriately was enough to set him off too if it weren't for his utter bewilderment.

"I don't get it" He spoke looking around for something else that could be the source of her amusement. Nothing. "What's so funny?" He asked.

"Oh nothing" The girl replied shaking her head as she pushed her sweatshirt sleeves up to her elbows "It's just that" The girl was interrupted by another attack of laughter before she composed herself enough to finish her sentence "It was only this morning that I was complaining to myself about how friendly the Americans are" she explained, lifting her hands to tug her caramel hair into a messy ponytail and climbing back into her car this time with her knee resting on the seat for an easier angle to try to dislodge the keys.

It was at this moment Mark realised the distinctive British accent the girl had as she returned to feeling blindly for the car keys in the small gap between the passenger and driver's seats of her car, muttering incoherent words of irritation as she did. What struck him the most though, wasn't her characteristic accent, but rather the clearly somewhat negative attitude she shared with him and it was this, for reasons Mark was still unclear of, that made him kneel down and open his tool box to rummage through just as irritably, until he finally found what he was looking for.

"Well" He drew out straightening up and moving away from his Corsa to the girl's MINI "I'm sorry to disappoint" he apologised without the slightest bit of sincerity as he pulled the girl from the car so that he could lean in himself. Surprised the girl let out a small sound between a gasp and cry when Mark pushed her back before swiping away the books hanging off the chair opposite him "But" He went on, carefully sliding the extendable magnet into the gap and sliding it from side to side until a satisfying clink came from the crevice "I'm not from America either" he told her, cautiously bringing the magnet back up, now with the lost keys attached and climbing back out of the car.

Triumphantly he held the keys up with a smug smile after pulling them away from the magnet before handing them to her and turning on his heel to return to his own vehicle.

"I'm from Taiwan"

CHAPTER FOUR

Alice

ALICE had, had her fair share of odd encounters both in Britain and America but this, she was sure, topped them all. It wasn't even particularly *weird.* Just. Very… Foreign.

Regardless of where she was, there was normally a set of social rules that were applied to any situation. Those rules varied from place to place but the entire interaction Alice had just experienced had been so… *unruly,* that anything Alice had *thought* she had learned about social interplay has been thrown out the window.

The Man had conformed to no set of typical mannerisms from any culture that Alice was familiar with and yet he had somehow moulded an impression of himself using only his actions anyway. He gave the influence of someone who once held a code of conduct of some sort in the past - otherwise he wouldn't have eventually helped her - but Alice wondered if he had somehow become estranged to it as she drove through the, now clear, road beside Washington State Park.

Curiously, Alice looked over into the green area to see if the commotion from that morning had left any settled dust but, much to her dismay, there wasn't even a blade of grass out of place as she passed the very same area, now devoid of any white tents, yellow police tape or indeed, police themselves.

For what felt like the thousandth time today, Alice huffed. She, like her father, possessed an uncanny ability to arrive just *after* something of interest happens, a trait she was well aware did *not* make a good journalist. One day she was sure she would be able to find a way to be in the right places at the right times but until then she would have to live with the near constant irritation and disappointment of always being left out of the loop somehow.

The whole series of events had left Alice so perplexed that by the time she had come to the quaint little café she had forgotten completely her craving for caffeine and instead habitually continued straight on to the high rise residential building her Aunt's apartment was situated in. It wasn't until she had pulled into her designated parking space in the building's underground parking area that she realised she had in fact driven straight past the very place she had intended to go to and bitterly she slapped her steering wheel, cursing her scatter-brained disposition. The whole day had been one irritating event to another. So much so, it was enough to send even a stable minded person mad, but Alice was already half mad with the amount of work she was snowed under with so what if you were already halfway there? Where was there to go?

As if sensing Alice's dangerously high levels of irritation her phone screen lit up in the cup holder beside her, signalling an incoming call. Calming quickly before she allowed herself to get into a state Alice scooped the device up quickly to read the contact name, only to let her head fall back against the cushioned headrest behind her. Her aunt, "generous" as she was, was the *last* person she wanted to talk to. Her neverendingly high levels of energy made Alice's own spirit flatline almost as if the woman was dipping into the supplies of others around her in order to keep her own topped up. All the same Alice still accepted the call, reluctantly lifting the phone to her ear.

"Aunt Isabella!" She spoke as cheerfully as she possibly could "You caught me just at the right moment" She told her glancing out the car window to the building entrance longingly. She may not have been able to get herself a coffee but at least she could have relaxed at home. However, a phone call from her aunt didn't bode well for that venture *either*. "I just parked at the apartment building" Maybe if she subtly hinted that she was winding down for the day then her aunt would pick up on it and leave whatever it was she wanted till tomorrow but even that was wishful thinking.

"Oh perfect!" Isabella responded completely oblivious to Alice's inconspicuous clues that, quite frankly, she wanted to hang up the phone and throw it across the length of the underground chamber she was currently in. If it were anyone else, Alice would have pretended that the signal wasn't good and ended it then and there, but her aunt would immediately catch on to the blatant lie. The apartment she was staying in was hers after all and when taking into consideration that Alice's aunt's phone was almost permanently attached to her ear, it was a safe assumption to make that

Isabella would know that the signal in the car park wouldn't make a difference at all.

"I was hoping you would be able to talk" She went on as Alice squeezed her eyes shut wearily. "Well, here I am!" She answered her face portraying the completely opposite emotion that her voice did. "It's nothing bad, don't worry" Isabella added quickly, seemingly picking up on Alice's slight tone of sarcasm the one time she *didn't* need her to "I just thought you would be interested in an internship opening with The New York Times one of my friends told me about this afternoon" Quickly Alice's eyes snapped open as she sat bolt upright.

Internships for aspiring Journalists were intensely competitive no matter where you went but to have an opportunity to get one at a newspaper as prestigious as The New York Times was rare as diamonds. "Really!" Alice exclaimed, all debilitation forgotten in her excitement "What section? How do I apply? When's the deadline?"

Isabella's bell like laughter resonated through Alice's phone speaker as questions spilled from her niece without even fully processing in her mind. "Calm down, Alice" She chuckled "Before you hurt yourself" Abruptly Alice closed her mouth biting her lip in anticipation. Oh, the things she could do with an internship like that on her CV. She could write for practically *anyone* once she finished her degree. "I've already applied *for* you" Isabella explained.

Alice's stomach plummeted through her seat and fell to the stone ground beneath her. Isabella was the *queen* of exaggeration. Lord *knows* what could have been put on an application form penned by Alice's exuberant aunt. She may have suddenly acquired ninja skills in the last two hours according the *Special Skills* section.

"You have?" Alice replied hoarsely, her mouth suddenly bone dry. "Mhm" Isabella hummed, as if preoccupied with something on the other end of the line "I spoke to my *other* friend, the News editor there. *Really* nice man, always so friendly" Nervously Alice bit down on her lower lip. Alice wasn't sure she wanted her potential boss' first impression to be one involving her aunt. "Anyway" Isabella interrupted herself, diverting back to her original point "He said you sounded like a very capable learner and if you want it, it's yours"

"Just like that?" Alice responded taken aback at the simplicity of it all "No forms or... or CVs?" she asked. It hardly seemed fair to someone else who might want to apply. "Well..." Isabella drew out "He wants to meet you tomorrow if you're free and you *could* draw up a quick CV, just to keep up formalities but between you and me, Alice. Joe owes me one. If he's a man of his word, this internship is in the bag"

Now Alice really *was* torn.

An internship at The New York Times was way too good an opportunity to pass up but something didn't sit right with Alice about the underhanded acquisition of said position. Apart from anything else it was disheartening to think that *Alice, hardworking student,* alone wasn't enough to get the internship and she had to resort to calling on favours from her aunt's connections, but at the same time… Isn't it just the same as accepting her aunt's gifts of roomy apartments and brand-new cars?

Swallowing down her guilt Alice nodded before remembering she was on the phone and the person she was in conversation with was not in the car with her and was in actual fact, nearly a thousand miles West, in Chicago. Awkwardly she coughed trying to figure out what to say before stammering out three measly words in reply.

"I-I'm free t-tomorrow"

CHAPTER FIVE

Mark

 MARK rarely stayed sober much later than seven pm, but tonight something about the hazy, nauseous experience of intoxication didn't appeal to him as much as it normally did. It might have been the thought of another pounding headache like the one he had endured for the majority of that morning or the fact that his limbs already felt like they were made of lead, but for once in his life Mark listened to his body. Shunning the shelf of cheap beer cans in his refrigerator, he instead scanned the remaining shelves for something that looked at least half edible and, after finding nothing, shut the door carelessly as he wandered back into the small living 'room' neighbouring the even smaller 'kitchen.' Mark sighed in a mixture of exhaustion and boredom as he collapsed onto the old sofa positioned under a small window overlooking the dark, dank ally way beside the large block of flats he lived in.

His sofa might have once been a dark shade of brown, possibly before he moved in, but from the day Mark had shifted all his things from his college dorm room in, it had been more of a hazel brown colour, after years of life in front of the miserable looking window. The wall directly opposite it was bare brick with a single canvas hung on it, above a small television. On it was a monochromatic painting of a dark, intricate butterfly. Mark guessed it was either ink or watercolour judging from the splatters and smudges that detailed the image, more likely the latter if you looked closer and realised the lines from where the colour, or rather - the lack of, had run.

To the right of the small living space, was a tiny kitchen area made up of a line of flat surface to prepare food on and cupboards that curved round to make a 'U' shape and section it off from the "living room" Pushed into the top left corner was a classic white fridge and beside it was a long line of worktop leading to a small cooker hidden at the far end of the rectangular shape made by the other surrounding worktops. Behind the white wall making the right-hand perimeter of the open plan living/kitchen space was a cramped bathroom with just enough capacity to fit a toilet with a small sink beside it and a two in one shower bath that had been squeezed into the small space available behind the back wall of a small cupboard beside the front door.

On Mark's left was another white wall with a single doorway leading into his bedroom. A simply furnished room with a double bed pushed into the corner left of the doorway along with a small IKEA bedside table at its side and a wardrobe positioned in the corner opposite, an old looking chest of drawers pushed up against it. Under the window of the far wall was a small desk with nothing more than a pot of pens and pencils and a lamp on its surface. It rarely got used and sat in the room in quiet solidarity much like the rest of the furnishings in Mark's flat.

The sofa, however, *always* got used. Much like it was being used today, with Mark sprawled across it debating whether or not the possibility of a headache free morning the next day was *really* worth the self-restraint he was displaying now. He was craving a hit of *something* that could take the edge off whatever it was he was feeling. Tired. Or maybe just run down? Were they the same thing? Gradually Mark's mind began to wander again as he stared at a red brick on the wall opposite him that had been chipped by a previous occupant of the modest living space.

Sometimes Mark wondered what had happened the day that dent had been made. Countless sleepless nights had been chased away with the stories of explosive arguments or fights that could have happened to explain the intriguing blemish left on the wall with just as countless endings, ranging from character deaths to major plot twists revealed in the heat of the moment.

Mark imagined a scene now. A domestic argument gone too far. Plates and photo frames hurled through the air until the girl's favourite lamp is smashed against the wall in a flurry of expletives and angry, personal insults by her boyfriend. "That was my favourite!" She would exclaim, suddenly sombre.

Mark wasn't sure why she felt the need to state the obvious. Her favourite could only be that lamp, it was the only one in the flat but he supposed that if you made out to have some sort of emotional connection to an object it seemed all the more heart wrenching to the one who had damaged it. An advanced form of guilt tripping, Mark would call it.

Suddenly the room would fall quiet with only the sounds of deep breathing coming from the girl's boyfriend preventing complete silence. His face would fall, realising what he had done; she would start to cry; he would try to apologise but it was all in vain. "Get out!" she would shout "Get out, get out!" It was loud again, except the roles had been switched. Now it was the girl who was angry and the man pleading with her to 'just let him *explain*' but it was all over in a flash as the girl shoved him out of the flat and slammed the door closed behind him.

Mark tilted his head as the girl began to fade from his mind's eye leaving him alone in the flat once again before glancing up at the clock hung above his bedroom door.

Mark was in for a long night.

CHAPTER SIX

Alice

ALICE lay in her bed and stared up at the plain white ceiling above her. Wide awake and with nothing more than the deafening silence of her aunt's penthouse to keep her company.

She didn't normally have trouble sleeping but tonight was different. Tonight, she had too much on her mind all at the same time. She still had two more assignments due in the next two weeks that she had planned on working on once she finally made it into the apartment earlier. Unfortunately, she was forced to push them all aside to pull together a subpar CV after her conversation with her aunt in the car.

She had just about managed to do it despite the fact that the old boiler her aunt had bought the apartment with had finally packed up, leaving the entire apartment feeling like a refrigerator in a power surge. It was tomorrow's meeting weighing on her mind the most, though.

Was it an interview or was it just a meet up to show the ropes like her aunt had implied? Should she dress for the office or more like the reporters you see in the movies? The questions were never ending.

And never answered either.

After two hours of restless thinking and deliberating and worrying. Alice gave up and climbed out from under the covers to wander down the dark staircase leading to the second tier of the apartment.

Isabella loved to entertain. So, it came as no surprise to Alice when she found that the apartment had *both* what her aunt had called a 'snug' on a second "gallery" level that looked down on an open plan living and dining area on the first level in addition to a large kitchen area concealed underneath the edge of the second floor.

As it stood, the bedroom and two bathrooms on the first and third levels were the only closed off rooms in the entire complex, leaving the apartment with a very exposing feeling. Particularly in the dark.

All the same, enough light from the New York City night life streamed in from the floor to ceiling glass window at the back of the apartment overlooking Seventh Avenue that Alice walked past the light switch as she made her way down the second set of stairs and moved straight into the modern kitchen area underneath the second floor gallery. It wasn't until she was already at the kettle positioned beside a matching coffee machine and coffee jug in the corner of the white work surface, that Alice realised the jar of instant coffee granules she had pulled from the shelf above had little more than half a teaspoon left in it. Not even enough for a cup.

Alice huffed putting the glass jar down carefully in her left hand but dropping its plastic lid from her right hand carelessly as she turned to lean back against the worktop tiredly. Across from her, the long dining table had papers and books strewn across it forming a halo of work and mostly useless text around her laptop as it sat, still open from where she had left it. Mockingly its lid peeked over the breakfast bar at her. An unwelcome reminder of all the work she hadn't finished.

 If she had, had a coffee earlier then maybe she might have thought twice before she climbed back up the stairs to her bedroom to change, clumsily in the darkness, into a pair of running leggings and her oversized NYU jumper that hung, half on, half off the stool in front of her dressing table. Alice was vaguely aware that it was the jumper she had worn two days in a row already, but she hardly cared. It wasn't like she was going to be traipsing around New York in the small hours. Her destination was only a mere two-minute walk away and she just needed something *other* than pyjamas to cross the road into the all-night coffee place over the street.

 It quite often baffled Alice as to why a coffee place would stay open well into the night hours when everyone knew it was the world's favourite stimulant. To consume the drink when one should be sleeping seemed preposterous, but it was tonight as Alice made her way across the busy road, laptop and books in hand, that she realised coffee shops stayed open for people like her. People who couldn't sleep and had nothing better to do other than keep themselves awake.

The combined aroma of bitter coffee and musky old books welcomed Alice as she entered the warm shop from the cold night air and behind a rustic looking wooden worktop, a barista looked up from an old looking science fiction comic book. Quickly the boy, eighteen, maybe nineteen, shoved the magazine under a stack of napkins and smiled at her ever so slightly, prompting her to step towards the counter.

"Um…" Alice drew out, scanning the chalkboard menu above the barista's head as he waited for her to decide "A… Caramel Latte" It sounded more like a question than an order but Alice didn't have the energy to read the entire menu. Most coffee shops would serve a caramel latte, right? It would seem silly *not* to. *'Just like it would be silly not to serve tea'* Alice had added in her head reminded of that awful tea she had got from the chain coffee shop opposite the Bobst Library.

This was no chain coffee shop, however. This was classic. Rustic. *Aesthetic.* It was both original and unoriginal at the same time. Because who's ever heard of a coffee shop using newspaper for wallpaper before? And having squishy, brown sofas with mismatched cushions, tucked behind small, unvarnished wood coffee tables. Or warm, atmospheric lighting coming from brass lamps and discreet hanging lights from above.

Everyone.

But somehow this shop made it, its own.

Alice realised that this shop was the exact opposite to the café she had passed earlier. That coffee shop was modern and bright and… *yellow.* This was comfy and neutral. Homelike. Alice almost felt like she was back in Britain sitting in her grandmother's front room as she chatted through the open kitchen door making tea. It wasn't home. She knew that. It was the home *feeling* and warmth and aromas as the boy began collecting various coffee things Alice didn't know the names or purposes of.

As expected, the boy nodded his head as he turned to the large professional coffee machine on his right. "You can find somewhere to sit and I'll bring it over to you when it's ready" He told her his accent a little less obvious than the police officer's Alice had encountered that day. A softer tone to it than the big bellowing of a lifelong Bronx resident or the nasal of someone from Queens. Perhaps not even from New York. She liked it. It was enough to separate him but not as obnoxious as most of the other accents Alice had come across.

Quietly Alice dipped her head before turning to the empty shop to look for a table to sit at. Most of the room was furnished with low squishy armchairs and sofas with just as low coffee tables that looked like slabs of left over timbre carelessly thrown together to make something out of it. Right at the back of the room, though, was a small two seater table sitting placidly in a dim corner. Perfect for someone alone.

And busy.

Quickly Alice put her heavy books and papers down on the tabletop and breathed a sigh of relief as her arms finally relaxed in the absence of the heavy load. The weight on her shoulders, however, remained just as present as she slid into the comfortable cushioned chair facing into the quaint café to arrange her books around her laptop before she opened the machine to locate her half-finished thesis on how profoundly Social Media has changed Journalism amongst the chaotic files saved to her hard drive.

Not ten minutes later the barista came over with a large glass designed to be the shape of a mug. In it was light brown, milky coffee piled high with whipped cream that almost toppled out of the glass as the barista placed it beside her carefully. "Oh, thank you" Alice spoke sitting up to look over the top of her laptop for her purse "H-how much do I owe you?" She stammered as she lifted up a stack of papers to her left to find the small leather pouch hiding beneath it. Quickly she snatched it up and unzipped it to pull out a five-dollar bill.

"Four dollars fifty" The boy replied shifting uncomfortably. Something told Alice that he preferred his spot behind the counter far more than the open space of the larger room, so she handed him the bill quickly, smiling gratefully as she told him to keep the change and let him scurry back to his comic so she could return to her thesis as the shop door opened, unexpectedly, for a second customer to enter.

CHAPTER SEVEN

Mark

The first thing Mark noticed was that when you first enter, it seemed like the entire shop was empty. Which was unusual. Giovanni, the owner, was normally very strict about keeping someone behind the counter at all times. The second thing he realised was that the shop wasn't empty and the only two other people in the room were just concealed in the far corner. Another customer, a girl, hunched over a pile of books and paper and a boy about the same age as her but definitely not the same league.

The boy was scrawny and lanky. All skin and bones with a good smattering of acne visible under a pair of wire frame glasses, but not the trendy, stylish type. The rectangular held together by tape type. The opposite to the type the girl beside him was wearing as he scuttled back towards the counter where Mark now stood waiting. Hers were round and golden, slightly too big for her and... familiar.

Mark frowned in concentration as the boy made his way back to the till, opening it up to place a five dollar bill before removing a fifty cent coin and dropping it in a glass jar labelled "TIPS" all the while he stared at the girl trying to recall if he knew her.

"Sir?" Mark blinked turning back to the counter "Is there anything I can get you?" Quickly he moved his hand to his back pocket, pulling his wallet out and looking up at the menu hung up on the wall despite the fact that he knew exactly what he was going to have. "Black coffee" He answered "Large" He looked up thinking for a moment before pulling out a second bill "Make that two" He decided.

Tonight, he was *not* sleeping, he had come to accept that, but he would rather not feel bored *and* tired at the same time. "Sure thing" The boy answered, "Is that eat in or takeaway?" Mark hesitated, glancing back at the girl now typing furiously at her laptop keyboard with a large textbook open beside her. Her bright blue eyes flickered between her screen and the pages making them sparkle in the white light drowning her. A sudden moment of realisation hit Mark. Like the blue orbs had somehow struck him with some magic lightning of knowledge and slowly Mark turned back to the boy his mind working at hundred miles a minute until impulsively and unexpectedly he blurted out "Eat in"

"Ok, that'll be five dollars forty" The barista replied pressing a few buttons on the till and taking the bills Mark handed him before returning the change he was owed. "You can find a seat and I'll bring your drinks over to you in just a second" He repeated as he turned away to begin making Mark's coffee, leaving Mark with no choice but to turn away from him also and scan the room behind him.

 He could just sit on the other side of the shop. Pretend he didn't know her at all and finish his coffee as quickly as possible, but that would defeat the point of coming out here at all. He was only here to burn the night away and rushing in and out wouldn't make a dent in the long night Mark had ahead of him.

The other option was to sit near her and wait for her to notice him, that is. If she recognised him at all and even if she did, it looked as if she was so engrossed in her work she wouldn't be looking around people watching anytime soon. So, slowly he started making his way to the other side of the room, heading for a small coffee table surrounded by two armchairs beside the large window before thinking better of it.

Mark didn't like large windows, in particular, being near them. They made him feel vulnerable and exposed. Like anyone walking past could and would be watching you, judging and anticipating your next action. Then again, that was practically the way of social interaction. A delicate choreography of one calculated response to another, equally, measured action depending on the situation one was in. Mark wondered if maybe that was why he wasn't very good at the whole social thing. His trust was not something Mark gave out often, in fact, since Jacob's accident, Mark hadn't trusted one person in the world, until he realised that his body had moved away from the window and further and further into the coffee shop before he came to a stop beside the one table in the entire shop that was occupied.

CHAPTER EIGHT

Alice

It took a moment or two for Alice to realise that the movement in front her was *intended* to grab her attention when the feeling of a presence opposite her lingered longer than Alice thought is should. Quickly she looked up from her work, expecting to see the barista standing over her for some reason or another. Perhaps because she had accidently given him less money than she thought but Alice jolted in surprise when a very different person entered her line of sight.

"O-oh!" She stammered, hastily pulling her glasses off and glancing at the barista who was otherwise preoccupied with his job. "I-it's you" Alice cringed at how disappointed it sounded but the man seemed distinctly unbothered by the somewhat rude tone she had used as he gave her a lopsided smirk. "That's not any way to greet an old friend" He replied before chuckling at his own joke. Any remorse Alice might have felt for her previous slip up melted away instantaneously.

"If by '*old friend*' you mean going back a maximum of eight hours, then sure" Alice answered narrowing her eyes almost imperceivably as the man, whom she realised she *still* did not know the name of, sat down opposite her. Uninvited but suspiciously more in control of the circumstances than Alice felt he ought to be. "Come on" He responded leaning forwards on the table to peer over the top of her laptop "I helped you find your keys" He reminded her.

"After much persuasion" Alice countered, setting her glasses down beside her computer so she could frown at the man disapprovingly "And I wouldn't call us friends after one cold encounter with each other" she added.

"I wasn't cold" the man defended himself, the warm light of the coffee shop glinting off of his dark hair as he shrugged seemingly untroubled by his bad first impression "I was hung over. There's a difference"

Alice eyed him warily. "You were hung over on a Thursday afternoon?" she repeated raising her eyebrows in yet more disapproval. "Hey, don't come after me for having interesting night habits when you're sat here at one o'clock in the morning too" The man pointed out leaning back in his chair looking smug when suddenly the barista appeared with two large coffees in his hands. Hastily he set them down in front of the man opposite Alice before heading back to his counter quickly, giving Alice a moment to ponder on what her new coffee shop mate had just said.

"Touché" She said finally as she watched the barista pull out his comic from under the napkins beside him once again "What's your name?" She asked saving her thesis document before shutting her computer lid and leaning over the table to rest her elbows on the edge of it. Slowly the man opposite her took a sip of his coffee as if considering whether or not he wanted to respond before setting his cup down and crossing his arms over his chest, almost like a protective barrier.

"Mark" He answered simply. Alice froze with her drink halfway to her lips. "Mark?" She repeated lowering her mug shaped glass. Mark nodded once. "I thought you said you were from Thailand or something" she said taking a sip from her drink before setting it down beside her. "*Taiwan*" Mark corrected.

"Right, right" Alice replied "Taiwan" She said looking at him expectantly and when he looked back at her blankly, she asked "Isn't Mark a little… Western?" Alice almost grimaced as she said it. Was she allowed to say that? Would he be offended? She never knew what she could and couldn't say these days. To Alice it seemed *anything, anybody* said could be turned into something offensive if someone tried hard enough but thankfully Mark didn't seem insulted in the slightest, laughing loudly at Alice's question before nodding almost to himself as he reached forward to pick up his coffee once again.

"That's because it is" He responded as if it were obvious, making Alice fidget, a jolt of humiliation shooting through her. Mark smirked as he watched her squirm over the rim of his coffee cup, taking his time to return it to its place on the saucer left in front of him.

"I have two names" Mark told her, making Alice relax slightly in response. Her bafflement being warranted was infinitely less embarrassing than it being due to a personal lack of culture literacy. At least there was a reasonably confusing explanation to match her perplexion. "A Taiwanese name and my English name. You guys seem to have a bit a trouble getting your heads around the pronunciation of my other one when I first moved over here" He explained smiling in quiet amusement.

 Unexpectedly, Alice felt a surge of confidence fill her. "Try me" Alice responded, almost as if she was out to prove something "What's your Taiwanese name?" Mark looked up at her in surprise for a moment before smiling at her for the first time… genuinely. "Liu Ming-Ha" He told her watching in enjoyment as she took a moment to process the new sounds before her face contorted in concentration and she opened her mouth to repeat his name very, very badly.

 Mark let out a sound halfway between a cough and a choke as Alice pursed her lips to contain her own giggles while blood rushing to her face made her cheeks burn in embarrassment, all confidence lost just as quickly as she had found it. Eventually her mouth betrayed her and, unable to contain it, one small chuckle escaped Alice's body, and another, and another until finally she was laughing almost as hysterically as Mark at her pitiful linguistic skills

"Ok, so it's a *little* hard" She admitted lifting her drink to her lips as if to hide behind it. "M-maybe just s-stick to Mark" Mark stammered through his laughter. "Hey!" Alice called out "It's not *that* funny!" It had the opposite effect. Mark howled with new uncontrollable laughter, clutching his stomach and it was like Alice's own laughter fed off of his. The harder *he* laughed, the more *she* followed suit. It was like a never-ending cycle of laughing, regaining their composure then setting one another off again. It felt like hours before they were able to return to normal conversation without being interrupted by a small giggle halfway through a sentence or between subjects. Eventually, though, Mark was able to regain functionality and leant forwards still smiling.

"So…" He paused looking over at her books "*Alice*?" Mark looked up raising his eyebrows in question as Alice nodded, desperately trying to stifle the last remaining giggles left in her before Mark went on glancing down at her books again. "Alice Valetine…What brings you to this coffee shop at such a late hour?" He questioned finishing his first cup of coffee and moving on to his second. Alice wondered if this was an accurate representation of how much coffee he consumed under normal circumstances or if he, like her, had been having a rough night also.

"Or early" Mark added lifting that second cup of coffee to his lips, his eyes already bright and simmering with caffeine from the last one. "Technically it's early" He stated glancing out the window on the other side of the room to his left. The sun had gone in long ago but the city was still very much awake with street and car lights creating a hazy, yellow glow on the darkened streets outside. Alice nodded, suddenly quiet at the reminder of exactly what she was trying to escape from.

"I couldn't sleep" She replied pushing away her mostly untouched Caramel Latte. It was too sweet for her liking but there was something so comforting about the idea of it that a normal cup of coffee seemed almost inappropriate. "I have assignments due and tomorrow I have a…" Alice hesitated. What *did* she have tomorrow? "Job interview" She settled. That was best the way to describe it, right? "*I'm meeting my new boss because my aunt helped me get a prestigious internship without even applying*" didn't sound too much better.

Mark sucked in through his teeth shaking his head. "Oh, the *joys* of college life" He replied sarcastically, making Alice nod in agreement. Oh, the joys indeed. Just thinking about all the work that she needed to do made her feel physically sick. Not to mention the work she'll have to do with this new internship. It felt like her life was gradually becoming one ever growing mountain of *work*.

"What about you?" She answered, turning the focus away from her "You must have a reason for being here too. What's your story?" Mark froze. It was only for a second, but it was long enough for Alice to notice. He didn't feel in control anymore… and he didn't like it.

"The same as you I suppose" He replied simply, bringing his free arm up to rest his elbow on the table in front of him, like a fence between him and her "I'm not very good at sleeping"

A heavy silence fell over them as they reached the end of their common ground and Alice struggled to find something to break the stiffness they had fallen into before it became unbearable. There was a duality in Mark that seemed to negotiate the mood of any one conversation he may be having and Alice struggled to adjust to his swings. It seemed he could go from casual and laidback dialogue to unsettling and intense quietness with the mere mention of a single word.

It made Alice's head spin with confusion. His mysteriousness and obvious retention of certain details made a part of her want to explode with personal and potentially intrusive questions while what remained of her screamed that this was *exactly* the type of stranger you're warned about as a child.

A moment or two passed as they sat in silence shifting uncomfortably from time to time until Alice glanced at the old roman numeral clock hung on the wall beside them. She gasped quickly gathering together her things as Mark sat up looking as surprised as Alice felt.

Three thirty. They had sat there for two and a half *hours* and in little over that time Alice would need to drag herself from her bed to get to her 'meeting' in time. "I'm sorry, Mark" She apologised as she snatched up her glasses and hastily pushed them up to the bridge of her nose "But I should really get back. It's late -…or early. Whichever it is. I need to get up in three hours or so and…"

Mark never caught the last of her sentence as the rustling of Alice's papers and the thump of her book closing drowned out her semi-incoherent gabbling. "Anyway, thank you for keeping me company" She went on obliviously, piling all her things into her arms precariously as Mark leant back to watch her move towards the door. "And who knows" She said slowing her pace suddenly as she turned back to him halfway to the door "Maybe we can do this again"

Alice almost chuckled. *Sit in an empty coffee shop with a stranger talking about everything and nothing until the early hours of the morning.*

Fat chance.

CHAPTER NINE

Alice

JOE Mitchell was every inch the "all American" stereotype. Even before Alice had met him, she could tell from the five by three-foot American flag nailed above his desk on the far wall of his office and his vast collection of bald eagle statuettes of varying sizes distributed across the rooms surfaces and shelves. Either he was exceedingly patriotic or he just had a vested interest in birds of prey indigenous to North

America. Alice suspected it was a little bit of both as she bounced her knee in nervous anticipation and her theory was only consolidated when "Joe" finally entered his office.

"Sorry about that" He apologised as he closed the glass door behind him. Alice raised her eyebrows imperceivably when she was taken aback by his relatively subtle Chicago accent. Compared to the intrusive harshness of most New York accents it was positively modest. One might even be able to describe it as soft but there was still that slight nasally tone that tied all American accents together. The sort of slant into the next word that every American accent, no matter where it's from, was based upon.

Joe was exactly how one might imagine a news editor at a big newspaper to be like. A middle-aged man with dark, greying hair, although, in all fairness to him, not quite at the stage of thinning. He possessed an odd combination of both sharp and soft features, like perhaps in his youth he had once been quite angular but had now been abated with age. While his chin was podgy and undefined, his nose has hard and pointed and slightly crooked.

'*From being broken once… or twice*' Alice thought as she stared at the slight bulge protruding from the side of his nose for a second too long to be acceptable.

Joe smiled warmly as he walked quickly to the other side of his large executive looking desk. He had the fast paced, purposeful walk of a man who was constantly moving towards a new task. Forever jumping from job to job. The sort of jumping that can nauseate and exhaust you at the same time and Joe's tiredness showed. It wasn't something physical, like a slouch. It was more a weariness hidden in his dull grey eyes.

Nevertheless, Joe seemed more enthusiastic about Alice being there than she was herself. Given the fact that Alice had, had no more than four hours sleep, however, it was a wonder that she was conscious at all. It had taken the combined effort of what was left of Alice's self-control and copious amounts of caffeine to get Alice out of bed and in the car. By the time she finally stumbled into the bright white, modern New York Times offices she was already feeling the effects of her coffee wearing off. She wished she could have another now and silently made a mental note to pick some up at the store on her way home to prevent yet another visit to an overpriced coffee shop.

"Some people just have *no* common sense" He explained ambiguously. Alice didn't ask what he meant by that. Something about his deliberate avoidance of names told her it was *meant* to be vague. "If you want something done you have to do it yourself, am I right?" Alice chuckled half-heartedly, enough to convince Joe that he had broken the ice but not so enthusiastically that she used up the last of her dwindling energy supplies.

"So, the famous Alice Valetine" He drew out pulling the thin manilla folder laying on his desk placidly, towards him. "I must say, at first I was a little surprised to get a phone call from your Aunt" He told her, speaking more like Alice was an old friend and not a potential intern "I had no idea she had a sister leave alone a niece" Alice smiled pleasantly, distinctly *unsurprised* at Joe's lack of knowledge to her existence. It wasn't his job to know of her and frankly, her Aunt is so isolated from the rest of the family here in America, Alice found it hard to believe that the subject of family was something she spoke about on regular basis.

"I only moved here six months ago. Most of our family live Britain so we don't see her often" Alice explained almost as vaguely as Joe had explained his lateness. "Ah, yes" Joe answered nodding as he preoccupied himself with Alice's mediocre CV in front of him "Yes, that makes sense" He mumbled, although Alice suspected that the last two sentences that had been said had almost certainly gone straight through one ear and out the other.

"Well, Alice" Joe said closing the folder after reviewing it for a grand total of two minutes. "Everything seems to be in order" He resolved as he pushed it aside. A part of Alice felt a little annoyed that she had spent nearly two hours last night seemingly for nothing but then again maybe it was better that he didn't spend too much time looking at the pitiful collection of bland and watery information she had managed to pull together. "Shall I show you who you'll be working with?"

Alice blinked. That was it. Joe hadn't even introduced himself, although granted both of them knew he didn't really need to. It still felt a little like this whole thing was on fast forward. The application process had been skipped entirely so now, what *should* have been a feature length movie, has been cut down to a meagre half hour long tv show. Alice didn't feel like this was an accurate representation of the real world at all.

Joe didn't seem to notice Alice's struggle to keep up with his break neck speed, however, and happily jumped up from his seat to walk around his desk once again with his fast, purposeful pace. He headed straight out of his office doorway, leaving Alice to quickly gather her bag and stumble after him into the hallway.

"Your aunt told me all about your course at NYU" Joe spoke over his shoulder as Alice speed walked to catch up "Congratulations on getting into NYU by the way" He interrupted himself before moving on before Alice had a chance to thank him in response. "Anyway I know you're particularly interested in *news*, news" Joe paused ever so slightly to wink at Alice as if he had just spoken a code she ought to know. "Not that crap in gossip magazines about celebrities diets and love lives" Alice hummed in response, although whether her sound indicated agreement or not was a mystery even to Alice herself.

"So, I've arranged for you to shadow Team Beta" Joe said, finally reaching his point as he stopped outside a glass door almost identical. For a busy man he didn't half *waffle*. It did give Alice a little comfort that *he* of all people was able to work his way up in a business based on people conveying information as effectively as possible when he clearly was not able to do so himself. Perhaps her inherently bad timing wouldn't be such a problem after all.

"Team Beta cover crime mostly, although there is a crossover into gossip when it's more high profile" He explained looking a little peeved at the admission as he opened the door.

Inside was a bright room made up of three pure white walls and one fully glass overlooking the busy street below them. Arranged in a large rectangle following the rooms dimensions and about three feet apart were identical black and white desks, each with a computer and various folders and papers on it's top. In the centre of the rectangle, placed strategically at one end to allow each reporter to see from where he or she was sitting, was a large cork board of various photographs, post its and strips of text, some of which were connected by red gift ribbon someone had clumsily pinned across the board.

Alice had often wondered if reporters really *did* use this method of investigation. She had, however, imagined something a little more glamourous than gift ribbon bought on sale from Target based on the large roll of it resting on the rail at the bottom of the board. Something about it wasn't as disappointing as Alice might have thought it would have been though and in fact the normality of it added a sprinkle of realness to the entire room. Like a pinch to make sure you weren't dreaming.

She was *here*. She was awake. She was a reporter. Or, at least, she was for the duration of this placement, but Alice was determined to soak up as much experience as she could from the people here. Be in the thick of it and learn every tip, trick, and tool a good journalist needs. She would prove to herself if no one else, that *Alice, hardworking student* was good enough. That she wasn't just *Alice, Isabella Thornton's Niece.*

CHAPTER TEN

Mark

IF Mark had slept at all last night he would have overslept the next morning and, for the first time in a long time, it wouldn't have been because he was so drunk the night before that he wasn't even sure if he was fully sober again when he woke up. But Mark hadn't slept last night, and he was still very much awake when the alarm on his out of date smart phone began ringing.

Mark let it ring for a few moments. Staring straight ahead of him from where he sat on his tidy, made up bed. He didn't remember coming back into his apartment after his second encounter with the girl he had met yesterday. He most certainly did not remember sitting on his bed for hours on end as time ploughed on without him but somehow that was exactly the position he found himself in the next time he had a conscious thought. He couldn't even remember the name of that same girl he had spent a majority of that same night with. He knew it. It was buried somewhere deep in that brilliant mind of his but all that he could think of were her *eyes*.

He was entirely consumed by them. How they were so out of place amongst all the unbroken brown and white that seemed to be the very *essence* of her and yet those eyes. Those sapphires, broke right through it all. They were engraved in his mind. Even now, hours after seeing them last, if he closed his eyes, he could still see them flicker in the harsh light of her laptop screen. He could still recall the *exact* shade of blue they were. A striking mix of sky and sea blue with a dark rim of intense colour around the iris like a bold outline screaming, '*Look at me!'* They were more precious than any sapphire Mark would have the good fortune to encounter.

But this was exactly Mark's problem. He obsessed. His father's illness had engulfed him, so had Jacob's death. Now this girl and her damned eyes was trapping him in himself just like all the other obsessions he had harboured at some point in his life.

This one was different though. It wasn't a bitter, angry fixation like those preceding it. It was fascination. Manic attraction threatening to send him over the edge.

He hated it. He wanted nothing more than to rip the feelings she made him feel away from him and throw them in a locked cupboard far, far away. Feelings were bad. Feelings meant pain. The sort he couldn't chase away with caffeine or alcohol. The sort he felt when Jacob and his father died all in one night.

The sort he felt *before*.

Mark shook the thought from his head quickly and leant over to pull his phone off of the bedside table and shut off the incessant ringing. Seven forty-seven…

Early.

Mark couldn't remember the last time he had been early. Come to think of it, Mark couldn't remember a time he had been *anything* but late. Especially after an all-nighter, which – granted – was most nights. Mark huffed dragging himself from the comfortable spot in the middle of the bed he had been sitting in to stand up too quickly. Immediately black spots exploded over Marks vision and clumsily he staggered to the side leaning heavily on his bedside table for support.

As if on cue, Mark's stomach growled so loudly that for a moment he thought he might have been able to see the sound waves rippling across his stomach. So much for listening to his body. Yesterday had been fuelled almost solely on caffeine and half of a left-over sharer packet of cheesy Doritos Mark had found in the back seat of his car around lunchtime. It wasn't any wonder why Mark felt like he had been run over by a bus and then reversed *back* over for good measure. He was running on no energy and zero sleep and yet it somehow made him feel more in control than when he had a full night of sleep and an even fuller belly.

A full stomach made him feel sluggish and slow and sleep made him paranoid. Instead Mark ran on anger. Motivation was hard to come by but the wonderful thing about anger is anything can give it to you. And when something is motivated by anger… It can run long. And hard. And brutal.

Mark relished the way his senses heightened when he was angry. How the colours around him were more vivid than before. The lights a little brighter. The sounds a little clearer. Sometimes his sense of smell and taste even merged into one and the smell of food stalls nearby would burst into explosions of flavour over his tongue without him so much as looking at them. It was a feeling no amount of food or relaxation could parallel.

It was *Mark.* Just like how brown and white and strange, misplaced shades of blue made up the girl he had met yesterday. Anger was at Mark's very core. An ever-present aura radiating from him even at his most composed. Mark could walk past you with nothing more than a blank expression and a heavy toolbox in his hand and you would still sense a quiet vengefulness in him. A fervid and unmistakable hatred for the world burned in his eyes, partially concealed in the darkness of their brown hue, but still very, *very* present.

Squeezing those dark brown eyes shut, Mark summoned as much energy as he could muster to push himself back up to his feet and stumble out of his room to the fridge. Just like last night, there was nothing but beer cans and half empty bottles of ketchup, mayo, and mustard inside and Mark didn't waste any time rooting through the empty packages he had left in there. Instead he moved straight on to the overhead cupboard beside it before suddenly remembering the only thing he would find in it was a cheap collection of plates, bowls, mugs, and glasses. Again, he stepped sideways to open the next cupboard.

Mostly filled with tins and cans of various foods and packages of dried pastas it took a large amount of rummaging through before Mark finally found a cereal box that wasn't empty. Peering inside he guessed there was a little more than one serving left of the sugary breakfast food before unceremoniously stuffing his hand straight into the box and raising a handful of the chocolaty 'o' shaped grains to his mouth. They tasted of nothing but sweeteners and sickly milk chocolate. A child's feast of sugar and excess energy in food form but Mark wasn't one to dwell on the quality or quantity of his food. As long as it chased away the dizzy nauseous feeling making his head spin for the next few hours he was satisfied.

And it did. After two or three more handfuls Mark could feel himself regaining his focus and put his new energy to use in prowling the kitchen to see *just* how empty his cupboards were, returning every once in a while to pull another handful of cereal from the discarded box on the counter. By the time Mark had finished his search he had found only four things left in his kitchen that were still in date, all of which were canned foods he didn't remember buying or even liking.

Reluctantly Mark made a mental note to stop at the supermarket on his way back from work as, baffled, he looked down at the can of black beans he had just pulled from the cupboard. Mark hadn't consumed even a morsel of the rancid vegetable since his mother had passed away before he moved to America and flat out refused to touch the stuff years after. Nonchalantly, though, Mark shrugged the confusion off. He didn't know how it had ended up in his kitchen. But he didn't care either.

CHAPTER ELEVEN

Alice

BY the time Alice staggered into her Aunt's apartment at the end of the day she felt even more wrung out than she had the day before, which was one of two new records broken today. The second, Alice was sure, was how much paperwork and shopping bags combined one could physically carry up ten flights of stairs.

Alice had left the New York Times building with arms piled high with paperwork the "real" journalists couldn't be bothered to do. It explained the Beta Team Room's unexpected delight when

Alice had been introduced as the new intern but as Alice arrived at her building to find the elevator out of order, it only made Alice's stress levels double in size. Multiple times on her way up the never-ending flights of stairs Alice found herself wondering if the name New York Times on her CV really was worth the pressure she was putting herself under. Her mountain of college work had already seemed impossible to get through before but now Alice's workload had become unfathomable.

Eventually, after many stops and starts, Alice managed to make it through the front door and into the dining area where she finally dropped the heavy folders on top of the long dining table carelessly. Quickly she leant forwards again though, wrapping her arms around the large pile as it threatened to spill over the already chaotic table before deflating over the table in a hopeless blob of congealed human being and anxiety personified.

"You know" A voice spoke from the front door followed by the sound of something brittle being snapped "You really should learn to manage your workload" The voice stated through a mouthful of food. Quickly Alice pushed herself up to half stand, half hang off the table enough to disguise her position as one of leaning rather than a desperate attempt to find stability in the closest structure she was to. Soon after, though, she dropped heavily into one of the chairs tucked neatly under the table, at seeing who exactly the voice belonged to as he moved into her line of sight.

"You seemed like you had a whole lotta work last night and this" Mark dropped a tool box at his feet and lifted his hand to let it fall heavily on top of Alice's second mountain of folders, casually taking another bite of the chocolate bar in his other "Was not part of it"

Wearily Alice looked up at him, half-heartedly attempting to smooth down her unkempt hair before giving up when she realised it was a hopeless cause and, frankly, the least of her worries. Suddenly she sat up as the absurd situation sunk in fully. Why was Mark Lee or Lim or whatever his last name was, standing, *uninvited*, in her apartment after no more than a day and a half since they first met and *how* in God's name did he know where she lived when she had no recollection of telling him herself anyway?

"H-how…" Alice trailed off looking over her shoulder to see the front door left wide open. "W-why…" Again she trailed off as she stood to move to the opening leading to the public hallway outside before shutting the door slowly.

"*What* are you doing here?" she asked turning to lean against the door handle and look back at Mark who was now consuming the last mouthful of his chocolate bar and pocketing the foil wrapper haphazardly.

"A-are you *following* me?" she questioned suddenly, silently cursing herself for indulging in his strange game of midnight tea parties last night.

Mark scoffed. "Don't flatter yourself" He retorted picking his toolbox back up and lifting it as if the action alone answered her question "Someone called about a broken boiler" He explained shortly.

Alice's mouth shut quickly, her body seizing up in humiliation. Of course, there would be a perfectly reasonable explanation for why he would be in her apartment. Of course, he wasn't some crazy stalker and *of course,* she would have to embarrass herself beyond compare by jumping to conclusions like she always did.

"O-oh" She stammered releasing the door handle slowly and straightening up in an attempt to keep what was left of her shredded dignity intact "O-of course" She answered, letting out a humourless laugh "That will have been, Ed"

Typical Ed. Organising for someone to come and fix something and not giving her any notice. Alice should have felt deja vu the moment she realised Mark in the doorway with his toolbox. "Um this way" She spoke moving past Mark to lead him out of the dining area and into the kitchen where the boiler was strategically hidden in a matching faux, dark wood cabinet to the rest of the kitchen cupboards. "It hasn't been working for the last couple of days and it's been starting to get cold" Alice explained, opening the cabinet door, and stepping aside so Mark could look the machine up and down from where he was standing two paces away beside the kitchen.

Dejectedly, Mark let his head fall back as an involuntary moan escaped his lips making Alice looked into the cabinet quickly. "What?" She asked worriedly glancing back at Mark as he quickly realised his mistake and lifted his head back up.

"Is it really bad?" She questioned anxiously. Alice didn't want to be rude but today had been exhausting. The idea of having another person in her house for much longer and having to play hostess was almost too much for her to bear when all she wanted was to collapse in bed.

"No" Mark replied.

He hesitated.

"Yes" He amended.

He pursed his lips.

"Sort of"

Alice's brow furrowed in confusion, any anxiety about Mark staying forgotten as she attempted to decipher his ambiguous response. "Look" Mark said, setting his toolbox down beside the kitchen island and moving forwards to point at one of the long copper pipes right at the back of the cupboard "You see the water running down here?" he asked, kneeling as Alice followed suit and sidled up beside him to peer into the cabinet also. "It means you have a leak somewhere in the pipe, probably at the joint and *that* means the water pressure isn't high enough"

Mark leant into the dark, enclosed space to look up from under the boiler. "No pressure, no heating" He concluded his voice sounding strained as he contracted his stomach muscles to keep himself up. "The good news is it's not hard to fix" He added observing the girl's, still, anxious expression as he pulled himself back to the bright open space of the kitchen floor. Alice's shoulders dropped down in relief and it took Mark everything in him not to smile too widely as he turned to drag his toolbox towards him from beside the island counter.

"Just long"

CHAPTER TWELVE

Mark

"WHAT is it that you study that gives you so much work anyway?" Mark asked.

He had been curious from the moment he had seen the heap of books strewn carelessly over the passenger side of Alice's car the day he had helped her retrieve her keys from the gap they had fallen through and his curiosity was only piqued further at seeing her working so late last night... Or early.

Technically it was early.

Alice looked up from her paperwork. "Well" Alice drew out when Mark turned away momentarily from his work to see her lifting her hand to rub her face before pulling it away hastily. "Shit" She interrupted herself as Mark returned his gaze to the appliance hanging above him.

"What was that?" Mark questioned from his lying position under the boiler. So far the only position that had allowed him to get anything done was lying on his back to look up at the boiler from underneath. Unfortunately, it meant lifting his arms up to reach even the bottom of the machine and after nearly an hour, his arms had gone past the burning that came with lactic acid and had moved on to state of almost complete numbness.

"Nothing" Alice replied quickly, standing and hurriedly moving past Mark to enter the first level bathroom to the right of the front door "Journalism" She answered Mark's question as momentarily the sounds of metal against metal ceased allowing Mark to hear the crackling of Alice deftly pulling a make-up remover wipe from its packaging.

"Journalism" Mark echoed, followed by the clattering of metal against metal once again "Isn't that just getting paid to spread rumours about overpaid attention seekers?" A moment passed before Alice reappeared now bare faced as she turned the bright white lights behind her off and moved back into the kitchen area. "Not the sort I want to do" Alice replied, dumping her used wipe in the bin stored in a tall drawer located somewhere to Mark's right.

Again, Mark's clanging stopped as Alice made her way to the other end of the worktop where her coffee machine was sitting in the corner, waiting to be used. "I want to follow crime stories. You know? Investigate and research and pin stuff up on a wall with red ribbon like in the T.V. shows" Alice huffed pulling an Americano from her new box of coffee pods she had remembered to buy on her way home. "So far all I've been made to do though is an eighty-page thesis and endless amounts of theory. Coffee?"

"Sure" Mark replied pulling himself out from under the boiler to check the pressure gauge. "Whatever you're having" Still low. Not as low as before though "What's all the shit for the New York Times then?" He asked giving the gauge a knock with the palm of his hand. Momentarily the thin needle under the glass face swayed from side to side before settling once again on the same number. "How did you…"

"There's a stamp on the top one" Mark replied, already anticipating what Alice was going to say as he straightened up and turned away from the boiler. "You should *look* at things more" He added taking the coffee Alice held out to him as she placed another pod in the machine beside her. "Maybe that way, you would have less questions" Alice hesitated, her coffee cup filling rapidly in front of her as she stood quietly. "Maybe you're right" she answered taking a deep breath before pulling the cup from under the machine and turning to lean back against the worktop, facing Mark.

For a second, Mark thought he saw a flash of sadness pass through her eyes and before he had a moment to think about it, guilt washed over him at the thought that what he had said might be the cause of it. Quickly he shook it off, renouncing once again any human emotion that tried to fight its way into his life.

Mark had let his guard down before. For a range of emotions; anger, agitation, lust even. But never guilt. The very word felt completely foreign in his mind let alone leaving his mouth. Which it wouldn't. But it was still there. Just a hint of it. But a hint was more guilt he had felt at one time than in the last two years combined.

"That stuff from the New York Times doesn't count anyway" Alice spoke up, perking up a bit "It's just paperwork that the *real* journalists can't be bothered with" Instantly Mark returned to his usual robotic state, any regret for his previous comment melting away at seeing Alice return to normal just as quickly.

"*Real* journalists?" He echoed frowning at the strange combination of words. What defined a *real* journalist? Were there journalists that were more real than others?

"Yeah" Alice replied sipping her coffee and flinching slightly when the heat burned her tongue "You know. The people who get paid to be there and *not* just gossip about celebrities" She explained "The people who get to investigate big stories about politicians and crimes"

Mark thought for a second, bringing his coffee cup to his lips before pulling it away quickly when his own tongue got scalded. "But" Cough "I-isn't that – I'm sorry" He interrupted himself as Alice quickly pulled some tissues off the kitchen roll standing beside her to begin clearing the coffee he had spilt. "I'll do that" He added taking the tissues from Alice after setting his coffee down, away from the big mess he had made. "Anyway" He returned to his original point "Isn't that what you do? Crime and politics?"

"*Want* to do" Alice corrected pulling more tissues away from the roll to help Mark despite the fact that he had almost finished mopping up the majority of his coffee from the worktop anyway. "There's a difference" Carefully Mark lifted the soaked tissues from the now clean worktop and moved towards the cupboard Alice had opened moments earlier to throw away her make-up wipe.

"Is there?" He replied dumping the tissues in the bin unceremoniously before stepping aside so Alice could do the same with her collection of sopping, dirty cloths. "If you want to do something why don't you just do it?" He asked closing the cabinet door after Alice had deposited the coffee stained tissues into the rubbish bin.

A moment of stillness passed as Alice's brows furrowed slightly and Mark chuckled quietly as he watched her expression of concentration. It was almost as if he could see the cogs in her mind whirring round and round to make sense of what he just said as he lifted his coffee cup to his lips once again. This time the coffee had cooled slightly and Mark was able to take a sip comfortably before Alice slowly began to nod, now leaning against the worktop in front of her.

"Yeah" she murmured nodding more confidently "Yeah, why *don't* I?" she repeated moving out of the kitchen suddenly and walking towards the pile of folders still stacked up leeringly on the dining table.

"What are you doing?" Mark asked curiously turning to watch her manoeuvre around the work top that separated the two living areas and start sifting through the folders carelessly, opening them one by one to the first page before closing them and sliding them into a new pile to her left. "I'm *doing*…Crime and Politics" Alice replied discarding yet another folder onto her new pile of what was clearly rejected options.

This time it was Mark's turn to be confused as he leant over the dark marble worktop to look over at what she was doing. "Doing, how?" He replied before realising that what he had just said made no more sense than Alice's previous statement. Surprisingly, though, Alice seemed to understand what he was trying to say perfectly and without hesitation hoisted half the pile of folders off the dining table and onto the worktop in front of Mark making him straighten up suddenly.

"These are all the potential crime leads the New York Times has in their files of tip offs" She explained turning back to the dining table to resume her hectic sorting "Have a look through and tell me if you think there's anything worth investigating" She instructed as she dropped another three folders in her discard pile, all at the same time this time and surprised by her sudden switch in mood, Mark found himself inclined to follow exactly as she had ordered, gingerly pulling a file from the pile in front of him and peering inside.

Almost instantaneously Mark started a discard pile of his own, sliding the same folder to the side to be forgotten along with many others to come. Over the course of the next half an hour or so Mark marvelled at how the New York Times had a crime section at all when all their leads were based mainly around missing pets and wayward teenagers. Folder after folder migrated from one side of Mark to the other, each with an equally preposterous or waste of time tip off enclosed, until Mark skimmed over a jarring photo taken in a sectioned off area in Washington Square Park.

Mark felt his eyes widen at the graphic photo as his eyes instinctively searched the photo for a date and sure enough, in the bottom righthand corner, a time and date stared up at him passively. The unusual shade of red made the distinctly digital characters seem to almost glow on the glossy photographic paper as Mark read and re-read the information he had found and gulped hard.

October 29th 2020, 11:45 am

Quickly he shut the folder and started moving it to the discard pile when he stopped suddenly, the folder hovering over the top of the pile in his half lifted, half lowered hand. Mark had friends, or rather people he knew that would be as close as he would get to friends, but they were a very different sort of person to Alice. They were reckless and careless and *loud.* Alice was the complete opposite and Mark wasn't sure if it was the weird juxtaposition they personified together or the disjunction she provided in his otherwise monotonous life but something drew him to her. Like the north pole of a magnet attracted the south the way they taught in his junior high physics lessons.

If it was him who found her first big story; he was involved. In any case he would be the only person Alice would be able to speak to about her investigations given that this was as close to plagiarism you could get without it *technically* falling under the definition of copying but *maybe,* just *maybe,* if it was his finding that started her on this path, his input would continue to be welcomed. He would have a new goal. A focus for the first time since he gave up his education.

Just as hastily Mark pulled his arm back and looked through the file once again.

It was perfect.

CHAPTER THIRTEEN

Alice

 WHEN Alice first decided to become a journalist she had envisioned a bustling, fast paced office of ever moving information, folders of photographs and first draft articles being passed from reporter to reporter for proof reading before being sent off to the editor at break neck speed. A far cry from the apathetic, lazy momentum of the Beta team room Alice now spent a majority of her time in.

Minute after minute ticked by on the bland white clock resting haphazardly on the coffee table beside Alice's small desk that was tucked in the back corner of the room as she made it look like she was busy. Beside her sat a slightly smaller stack of folders filled with old articles ready to be filed and archived. Secretly Alice hoped this would be the only job she would be tasked with doing whilst she continued her internship at the New York Times. Or at least until she finished what she had started.

A week had passed since the night Mark had come to fix her boiler and then subsequently became involved in a partially illicit search through what *should* have been strictly confidential files belonging to the New York Times. Normally Alice would have been mortified that the thought of breaking the rules with so little care for consequences had even crossed her mind but what Mark had said that night made something click.

Alice had spent years sucking up to people and working hard to finish task after task she had been given to the best of her ability.

And that was exactly her problem.

She always waited for something to be *given* to her. She never just *took* something. Grasped an opportunity with both hands and held on to it. Being a journalist wasn't about good timing or even a sharp eye. It was about luck. Specifically making your own. That night when she had been given all those fresh tip offs ready to be investigated, was an opportunity. To prove herself. To prove she could follow a story. To prove she had what it takes to be a true investigative journalist.

Alice did find herself feeling uncharacteristically in the wrong when she handed the freshly sorted stacks of files back with one missing the following day but as each shift crawled along and Alice found herself bending more and more rules to dedicate more time to her own project in work time. She found herself growing more and more numb to the feeling of guilt.

Soon she had developed a furtive system of completing just enough work to avoid detection by her superiors and still leave most of her time to commit to something far more fascinating and exciting than the blandness of entry level office work.

Alice looked down at the case file she had hidden in plain sight among all the other folders strewn across her desk. She had known as soon as Mark had slid the open folder over to her that night that it was a sign. Or perhaps the previous morning had been the sign and this is what it had been pointing to because for the first time ever; Alice had been in exactly the right place at almost exactly the right time. The moment Alice took in the explicit photograph she knew she had already answered one of many questions she had.

That this was what the strange white tent in Washington Square Park yesterday morning was concealing.

Forensics.

And crime.

And one very, very dead girl.

Bruised and bloodied as she lay on the disturbed area of grass; unmoving, almost sorrowful, and yet Alice found herself feeling not sympathy for the girl but rather an almost morbid fascination. Something about the violent act encapsulated in this one photo drew her in. Something amiss. There was something drastically different about this crime than any other of its cousins. It was messy and careless and... *impulsive*.

Alice couldn't understand why she had been left so exposed, in the middle of an open space like Washington Square Park. She would be discovered almost immediately and any forensic evidence found on the body would surely lead the police straight to her killer. Yet there she was. A beacon of drama, attracting attention like moths to a flame.

Alice *had* in effect "stolen" the tip off from Beta team but she was still surprised they hadn't picked it up elsewhere it was so obvious. Their office hadn't so much as mentioned the fact that a dead girl had been found not three miles away in plain sight. So Alice continued to quietly deceive them as she delved deeper and deeper into the peculiar mystery.

Alice was drawn from her thoughts suddenly, however, when her phone vibrated and quickly she glanced around her before discreetly pulling the small machine from her trouser pocket, being careful to keep it concealed under her desk and out of sight. On her screen a bright notification box concealed some of her home screen photograph to bring her attention to a text message she had just received and immediately Alice tapped the message icon to open it up fully.

Evelyn, 5:04pm
You. Me. Club. Tonight. No excuses.

Alice pursed her lips. She loved Evelyn like a sister and they had immediately clicked when they first met in their shared university lectures but there was one thing about Evelyn she could only bring herself to *tolerate*. For the sake of their friendship.

Her insatiable thirst for nights out and not just your average student's type of night out. Evelyn's sort of night out. Which more often than not ended in Alice half carrying, half dragging Evelyn back to her college dorm in the small hours of the morning.

Not what Alice wanted tonight.

It wasn't that Alice was particularly tired, it was more that she wanted, no, *needed* to keep looking into this murder. Question after question had been piling up in her small pocket-sized notebook she was using to store her findings but no answers were coming to light for her to match. Each night Alice convinced herself it would be that evening something would click into to place and each night she hit another dead end. She was sure that if she only did a little more research she would find something that would shift the whole case into gear for her. It was just a question of how much more.

Alice, 5:06pm
Sorry. I've got plans tonight. Maybe another time? Xx

Immediately three dots at the bottom of Alice's screen indicated that Evelyn was typing back and it wasn't long before they were replaced with a single, frank word.

Evelyn, 5:06pm
Bull.

More dots before another, longer message appeared.

Evelyn, 5:07pm
Alice Valetine. You NEVER have plans unless I make them for you. I love you dearly but you're like a social hermit.

Alice considered her friend's message for a moment. It was a bit brutal but she couldn't deny the accuracy of Evelyn's words. Alice's normal behaviour would lead *anyone* to believe that she was in fact a hermit. When all she did was travel between school, work, and her home with the occasional visit to a coffeeshop, it *was* hard to deny the use of the words "social recluse" in any given description of her but in this particular situation… It made it very, very hard to lie.

Alice 5:07pm
Well I do.

Quickly Alice typed out a second message before Evelyn had a chance to reply.

Alice, 5:07pm
I have a date.

A moment of technological silence fell over the pair of friends. So long that Alice even checked to see if Evelyn was still online when all at once message after message came through, ranging from moving images of excited people jumping around and party popper emojis.

Before the first coherent message drifted onto Alice's screen she had received a total of four moving images, three lines of random jumbled up letters and at least six different combinations of various party and excitement emoji's.

Evelyn, 5:08pm
Shut up! Shut up! SHUT UP!

Alice smirked at her small victory over her friend.

Alice, 5:08pm
With paperwork.

Once again Alice's phone was attacked with a string of messages from Evelyn. This time conveying quite the opposite emotion to excitement and comprising of mainly expletives only Evelyn would know and use. Evelyn was quick to return to the main concern at hand, though. Which was, currently, her jeopardised late-night plans.

Evelyn, 5:09pm
You are coming out with me tonight, End of.

There was a pause as Evelyn waited for a reply and Alice once again searched her mind for a pre prepared excuse to wriggle out of this one and when nothing came Evelyn tried one last tactic usually reserved for when she was *truly* desperate to drag Alice from her social cave.

Evelyn, 5:10pm
You deserve a break from all that work you do anyway.

Alice hesitated.

Evelyn had used this trick a thousand times before but maybe this time she was right. Maybe she *should* take a break from all the work she was doing. Busying herself constantly with her new investigation had taken its toll and as every day progressed and Alice studied what she already knew of the case for what felt like the thousandth time, the facts became more and more jumbled in Alice's mind. Perhaps if she walked away and came back again with fresh eyes everything would become a little more focused.

Alice, 5:11pm
Ok. But ONLY until 12.

CHAPTER FOURTEEN

Mark

MARK hated this club.

In fact. Mark hated most clubs. There was always too many people in not enough room but unfortunately, it appeared to be the only past time his so-called "friends" weren't vehemently opposed to. Aside from a few other significantly more illegal activities. So, Mark tolerated it. If nothing else, for the free pass to drink as much alcohol as he could afford and this Friday night, like most Friday nights, Mark found himself sat round a large table piled high with empty glasses and half-drunk drinks with six other rowdy, drunk young men.

Two of the group, Sam, and Robin, were the same age as Mark and had recently graduated from NYU in the same class that Mark would have graduated from, had he not dropped out. Kit, however, a seemingly clean-cut international student from Britain, was still in his first year at NYU but as much as he possessed the allurement and charisma of a modern-day Prince Charming, Mark knew as well as he did that his studies had gone down the drain ever since joining their dysfunctional and disruptive group of wayward hooligans.

He and Hunter were the two youngest of the group with Hunter only having turned twenty in the last month and Kit still only nineteen. The rest, Jay and Eli, were both two or three years older than the rest and both were burn outs working dead end jobs, like Mark. Jay and Hunter managed to get by working in their Dad's old car garage. Where the group sometimes gathered on nights when money was tight for each of the lads but a crate or two of beer was still affordable. Jay, being the oldest of the group, was usually the ringleader as well as, Mark suspected, the leading reason for their less than perfect reputation.

It was obvious that no other group had been comprised so completely of instinctive Alpha males and clashes of dominance were common within their network of what would be better described as *alliances* than *friendships*. Jay and Eli, however, were particularly brusque and reckless. Perhaps it was because they had been getting into trouble together for so long that the thrill of breaking the rules had become ineffective to them or perhaps they just didn't care enough for there to be a thrill at all anymore but both seemed to find trouble even if they weren't looking for it.

Sometimes it came in the form of a fight, other times it was a drunken decision landing them in trouble but how they got there wasn't really of any great importance. It was how they managed to drag the rest of their friends down with them that was extraordinary.

The first time it was Jay's younger brother who blindly followed them into a fight that wasn't his. Hunter might have done well in life if it weren't for his brother. Jay had no idea his brother was handy in a fight, until that time Hunter bailed him and Eli out, that is. It might have stayed that way as well, if Hunter had just stayed out of his brother's problems. Hunter, though, smart as he was, held family loyalty over self-preservation.

Jay had been dragging him into a world of violence ever since and it wasn't long before even more young men found themselves joining them in their illicit exploits across the city. Some had been sucked in by loyalty, like Hunter. Most simply found themselves in the wrong place at the wrong time, like Sam and Robin but Mark was the only member of the group who hated spending time with them as equally as he liked it.

After Jay and Hunter had paid the debts his father had left behind when Mark had no means to and Jacob had put him in contact with the two brothers, Mark first started fighting their battles out of obligation. He continued to fight out of addiction.

Once he had got that first, unique taste of violence, Mark had been desperately chasing after the electrifying rush of adrenaline that came with breaking the rules so, alongside Jay and Eli's band of urban misfits, he had drunk until he couldn't see straight and vandalised each private land they trespassed on. To no avail.

No matter how many train sides he defaced or cans of beer he threw down himself, Mark still went home feeling restless and empty. His mind perpetually void of any thoughts but still moving a thousand miles a minute and his hands twitching in idleness.

A part of Mark felt ashamed that he continued to keep company with them. They were, after all, the reason that Jacob was dead and his motives for remaining in their circle were nothing short of selfish and greedy but Mark was too deep into their, no, *his* way of life, to give it up now. Mark may be party to their crimes but there were parts of his life that were still his own. Mark just wondered if that was better or worse than having it the other way around.

The thumping, pulsating music crashing around the darkened room Mark remained seated in, however, made it hard for any thought to cross his mind other than whether he was likely to leave this building with his hearing intact or not. Still, Mark made no move to leave as he tried to decide on whether he valued his senses or his drink more and, opposite him, Kit downed his third shot of the night while the rest of their friends watched on, cheering in delight when half of it was spilt on the table top in front of him. The night was still too young for him to stomach strong drinks like that by themselves.

But not young enough for Mark to stay any longer.

Briskly, Mark stood and turned to begin moving away from the booth the group had claimed for the night, causing shouts of confusion and annoyance to come from everyone behind him but Kit who was still swiping at the tequila sliding down his chin. He ignored them, heading straight for the exit when suddenly he stopped in his tracks, not two strides away from his table.

Right there, no more than ten metres away on the other side of the room, a girl wearing a tight, pitch black mini dress made of a shiny satin fabric pushed through the crowds from the entrance with her friend following after her closely. The second girl wore a similar dress except with a more modest cowl neckline than her friend's deep plunge. What caught Mark's attention, however, wasn't the revealing tightness of the sparkling sequined dress or the indulgent shortness of the garment.

It was the fact that it was worn by someone he knew.

Someone *not* in the group behind him.

And it was the first true colour he had ever seen Alice wear.

CHAPTER FIFTEEN

Alice

EVELYN was almost the exact opposite of Alice. Everything about her was more… extreme.

And strikingly beautiful.

Alice's hair was a warm, neutral shade. Somewhere between blonde and dark brown. Evelyn's was jet black. As dark as the evening streets of New York City they had walked through moments ago and while Evelyn shared the same, pasty, almost death-like, complexion as her friend; small areas of pink on her cheeks and nose pushed through her otherwise wax like skin, giving out a small sign of life from within the vampiric girl. Normally, Alice appeared blotchy and flushed when any sort of colour came to her face but Evelyn's skin was never anything short of perfect. Without a blemish in sight, her skin clashed brilliantly with the darkness of her hair and shadowy brown eyes.

Monochrome worked for her.

The very discord of dark and light that seemed to overshadow Alice made her friend radiate refinement and grace. It made Alice envy a whole throng of characteristics Evelyn possessed and Alice could only wish she had.

Even now, as Evelyn glided across the dance floor to the only open area beside the bar of the club they had just entered, Alice found herself desperately yearning for a pair of never-ending legs like hers. Not least, so she could stop having to scurry after her friend on her significantly smaller legs to keep up.

"What are you drinking?" Evelyn asked, pulling out her purse as Alice caught up to her at the bar and tugged the hem of her sparkling, wine red dress down irritably. "I told you I should have got the size up" She grumbled quietly as Evelyn pulled out the fake ID card she had somehow acquired in her first week at NYU, much to the disapproval of Alice.

"Don't you guys virtually *encourage* under-age drinking where you're from?" Evelyn had questioned defensively, the first time she had used it.

"That's not the point" Alice had replied just as shortly "At least we get someone the right age to *buy* the stuff"

But Evelyn had made a good point. Not *every* British person broke the law the way Evelyn had described, by any stretch of the imagination, but Alice *certainly* didn't have a leg to stand on. So, she let subject drop fairly quickly and soon the card blended in with any other Evelyn had stowed away in the ever-growing purse of loyalty cards and coffee shop stamp collections she held now.

"And look like a potato sack" Evelyn responded sarcastically, turning back to the bar when a young bar tender made eye contact with her "You're better off not buying the dress at all than making it look like a twelve-year-old made it" Alice resisted the urge to point out that in actual fact she *hadn't* wanted to buy it in the first place and the only reason it happened to be in her mainly casual wardrobe was because *Evelyn* had insisted she needed at least *one* party dress to get her through her college days.

"What can I get you?" The man shouted over the loud thumping music as he leaned over the bar area to hear Evelyn better as she ordered "Can I get a vodka and coke and…" Evelyn paused glancing at Alice who momentarily stopped fiddling with her dress to look up at the barman looking to her expectantly "Just a coke" she requested before quickly adding "Diet. A diet coke please"

Silently the barman nodded before turning to start preparing their drinks as Evelyn looked over at Alice disdainfully, sliding the fake ID back into her purse. If she hadn't been asked for proof of age yet then she wouldn't be anytime soon. "Honestly, Alice" She spoke as if she were speaking to a child who didn't know any better "You really need to lighten up a bit"

It was at this point Alice felt a wave of relief that she had remembered to bring her car as an excuse to remain sober. Alice could sometimes drink Evelyn under the table but that didn't mean she was up for it every time they went out. The past week had taken it out of her and Alice suspected that, that, combined with the extreme lack of sleep she was suffering from and extortionate amounts of alcohol, wouldn't be too hard an equation to solve.

 Suddenly, a shout from across the room, however, saved Alice from having to think of an acceptable response. She and Evelyn turned in curiosity to see who had made the noise and, quickly, they located a group of young men no more than two or three years older than themselves causing a commotion from the secluded booth they sat in as one of their number turned on the dance floor and moved hurriedly towards the group with his head bowed low. Each of the men wore confused expressions as their friend re-joined them, shoving one of them out of his seat to sit down facing away from the room, the bright lights of the club glinting off his dark, glossy hair.

 He was almost like a male version of Evelyn, except with less pasty skin and a more honey like complexion. Warm and dark and obscure, not extreme, and blazingly silvery like Evelyn's. With Evelyn, everything was laid bare. This man was inviting interest from how little he gave you. He seemed designed to draw you into his mystery. He was…

 "Mark?" Alice mumbled squinting to see the figure more clearly in the entanglement of darkness and flashing lights but, hard as she tried, the only thing Alice could make out was the back of his head as he and his friends now spoke secretively around their table. Baffled, Evelyn lowered her head to follow Alice's line of sight to the table of friends and frowned when neither she could identify any one of them.

"Who?" She asked. Unexpectedly the man glanced back at them only to turn back to the table so violently he almost swivelled a full circle back round the other side of the chair he was sat in but that quick glance was all Alice needed to catch a glimpse of Mark's angular jaw line and sharp, intense eye shape. "Do you know that guy?" Evelyn questioned, handing the barman her debit card.

"Yeah" Alice replied turning back to Evelyn to take her drink from her. "No" She corrected. "Sort of" Alice spoke the last two words as if they were more of a question than an answer and Evelyn raised an eyebrow in suspicion. "Pick one" She told her friend before she took a sip of her drink tentatively to avoid the contents of her glass spilling over and taking her debit card back from the barman. Evelyn turned to give Alice an unamused look "Either you know him or you don't. You can't really have an in between with these sorts of things"

Alice huffed. "There is with *this* guy" she grumbled as she recalled what it was like trying to talk to him "I *know* him as in I know his *name* but that's it" Alice cut her hand through the air between her and Evelyn to make her point clear "That's *all* I know about-"

"No" Evelyn interrupted, lifting her hand to stop Alice speaking as she quickly swallowed the mouthful of vodka and coke she had just taken. "You also know that he's drop dead gorgeous *and* sitting right over there" she stated matter-of-factly putting her drink down to forcefully spin Alice around and nudge her towards Mark's table for good measure. "So pick up your drink and go and *talk* to him" Immediately Alice spun back round, moving back to the bar top as if it may provide some sort of shelter from Evelyn's unexpected attempts to broaden her social life once again.

"I can't go over there!" she exclaimed holding onto the bar stool in front of her like an anchor. "Didn't you see?" This time it was Evelyn's turn to huff. "See *what*?" she responded crossing her arms, unamused. Alice glanced over at Mark self-consciously before leaning closer to Evelyn.

"He didn't want me to see him"

CHAPTER SIXTEEN

Mark

THIS was too close. Having both sides of his life confined to one small room, packed full of people, was too unbelievably, dangerously close. Mark needed to remove himself. Before he became the crossing over the chasm that divided the two sectors of his world. Having Alice know the people he spent time with, or moreover, having the people he spent time with know Alice, would only end in one way.

Disaster.

Her life would be permanently destroyed after she inevitably got tangled in their web of skulduggery and any bridges he had managed to build with a normal human being would go up in flames. He couldn't risk that. He needed to keep them separate.

Yet again, Mark found himself feeling something other than anger for the first time in two years and he found it hard not to fidget in his seat as his desperation to leave began to replace his bitterness and he scoured the club for a quick escape. One where he could disappear into thin air, preferably. Without a trace. But unfortunately, it appeared he would have to settle for the next best thing.

"Jay" Mark hissed across the table, still careful to keep his back turned to the room. Quickly Jay turned to Mark and silently he tipped his head towards the figure who had just walked past them. Almost immediately a dark scowl cast shadows over Jay's face and wordlessly he stood to move past Mark, who also rose to his feet in order to follow the older man towards the exit.

Deftly Mark glided through the heaving masses of people, his eyes locked onto Jay in front of him as he twisted and turned his body to slide through the small spaces available to move through. He could already feel the familiar tingling of anticipation as it spread across him. Like a cloud of hot sparks hurtling into each other as the mass of the little balls of energy slowly crawled over each muscle just under his skin.

Mark's heart skipped a beat when he stepped out of the building and the crisp night air collided with the warmth of his body like a ton of bricks and hot and cold clashed explosively. Adrenaline pumped through his veins as he looked to his right for Jay and the other man when a voice made him snap his head to the left.

"Erik" Jay spoke nonchalantly, as if he were merely speaking to an old friend. "Long time no see." Immediately the man in front of him stopped in the middle of the abandoned backstreet the club led out to. "You haven't been avoiding me have you?" Erik questioned, turning slowly, and smirking as Mark moved to stand at Jay's flank. He knew a fight was coming. He could smell it in the air like a wolf could smell its prey in the wind from miles away.

And he wanted in.

He wanted nothing more than to throw a punch and have one come back. To feel the bruising collision of knuckles against his jaw, if only for a reason to do the same. To feel the warm viscosity of blood as it rolled from his nose and over his lips, leaving a bitter, metallic taste in his mouth. To see the animosity in his opponent. And to feel it in himself.

Mark felt *himself* when he was fighting. It was the most basic of instincts, to protect yourself, and Mark spent so much time repressing as much of himself as was humanly possible that he welcomed the opportunity to shut off his ever-moving mind and follow his body that violence brought to him. There was no thinking. No decisions being made. Just action.

Jay chuckled lifting his hand to run a hand over the short induction buzzcut he currently had. About a month ago he had no hair to speak of after Eli had drunkenly taken some clippers to his head in the small hours following the emptying of two crates of beer between them. It had since grown back a little, however, leaving Jay with the uneven, dark shadow of a man who was bald by choice across his scalp. "You wish, Erik" Jay replied, his face shifting quickly from a breezy, unbothered expression, to one of unmasked hostility. "I think you owe me some money"

Erik's smile didn't waver but the shower of light drowning him from the streetlight above him cast dark shadows over his face from his brow bones resulting in a more manic than friendly projection radiating from the already famously unbalanced man.

"For what?" He countered "Some dodgy pills padded out with who knows what?"

"Padded or not you bought them and I want my money" Jay responded flatly. Mark supressed a smile when Jay swerved the allegation Erik had made and pulled the conversation to a more inflammatory subject. He knew Jay would never throw the first punch. Neither would he. Anyone with half a brain knew you never threw the first punch. If you did you can kiss your self-defence plea goodbye. Thankfully, though, Erik possessed neither common sense nor patience and would probably find a fight in an empty room of padded walls given the opportunity. If he was pushed far enough Mark and Jay would get what they wanted soon enough.

"I 'ain't giving you anything" Erik spoke lowly, his smile disappearing to mirror Jay's dark expression before he turned on his heel and strode out of the light he was under in one smooth movement. "That's not what your girl was saying when she was all over me the other night" Mark called after him.

Beside him Jay coughed into his hand, in an effort to conceal laughter as Erik froze mid step and turned back to the pair of young men with a grave look on his face. "She couldn't keep her hands off me" Mark taunted knowing full well that it was a gross exaggeration of the truth. Parts of what he was saying were honest. Erik's current flame wasn't one to let herself be "tied down," for want of a better phrase, and Mark *had* encountered the girl's double-crossing antics no more than two weeks ago. What he failed to disclose, however, was that it wasn't him she had been trying – and failing - to seduce, but rather, young Kit who, very quickly, sent her on her way. Mark was no snitch though and besides; Kit hadn't come out tonight looking for a fight. Mark had and this was him finding it.

"You wanna say that again to my face?" Erik responded aggressively, his fist clenching at his side. Mark smirked insolently before stepping forwards to move past Jay and stand so close to the older man that their noses were nearly touching. "Your girl's a slut" he murmured.

Erik's fist came so quickly that Mark barely had enough time to register what was happening. Violently his head snapped sideways as Erik's knuckles slammed into his jaw and a grunt left his lips when he stumbled heavily into the wall beside them, breathing deeply.

A moment passed as Mark propped himself up against the wall and slowly lifted his hand to his lip before pulling it back to see blood smeared on his fingers. Leeringly, Erik stood over him, slumped against the heavily graffitied bricks, a victorious smile growing on his lips only for it to be replaced with an expression of shock when Mark lurched forwards and tackled him to the ground.

All at once, the odds had been turned as Mark landed a devastating blow to his opponent's jaw, identical to the one he had received moments earlier. Punch after punch from Mark landed with mortifying effect and morbidly he savoured the feeling of the delicate skin on his knuckles splitting and each shattering blow ricocheting up his arms. From behind him, Jay egged him on with shouts of encouragement and taunts aimed at the more disadvantaged of the pair when white exploded over Mark's eyesight, blinding him.

Pain seared across his temple as Mark hit the ground and Erik took the opportunity to sit up with his hand raised high, clutching a bloody, jagged piece of brick. Again, the tables had turned and for one unsure moment Mark thought Erik might hit him again. It wasn't long, however, before Jay had joined the fray, locking Erik's thick neck in the crook of his elbow, and dragging him a foot or two away from where Mark lay on the ground in a daze.

Each heartbeat made Mark's head pound as he desperately fought the urge to bring back up the little food he had consumed since lunchtime and warm, sticky blood began to slide down the side of his face. Somewhere in the fuzzy cacophony of noise Mark could make out Jay, calling out his name, but everything was too out of focus for him to match the body to the voice until he was directly in front of him, grabbing Mark's shoulders roughly.

"Mark. Hey, Mark, can you hear me?" Jay asked, shaking him carelessly as he searched the younger man's features worriedly "How many fingers am I holding up?" Blearily Mark looked up from the ground to squint in the vague direction of where Jay's voice was coming from until he finally found the blurred outline of Jay's fingers and carefully he began to count them until something moving in the unfocused background pulled his line of sight away from Jay's mysterious eight fingers.

"A-Alice?" Mark stammered frowning when the blob of deep, wine red began to focus more as it grew closer and closer. "You've lost your mind, Mark" Jay replied true worry seeping into his eyes

"How hard did he hit you?" Mark pushed Jay aside, ignoring his question as he pushed himself to his feet unsteadily "Alice what are you doing…"

"I could ask you the same question" The girl interrupted, her face contorted in an expression half-way between fury and concern "Starting fights in alleyways and almost getting yourself *killed*" Mark blinked in surprise still trying to process her very presence at the scene of the crime let alone what she had just said. She was supposed to be inside. She wasn't even supposed to *know* he was *here* and yet here she was, scolding him for getting into a scrap.

"I…" Mark trailed off unsure how he intended to finish the sentence he had started before he finally let out the only pathetic phrase he could think of.

"I'm not dead"

"Too right you're not bloody dead but you *are* bloody, *bloody*!" Alice exclaimed tugging at the shoulder of Mark's white t-shirt that had now been doused in the bright red liquid streaming from the side of his head. Mark smiled at how Alice seemed to become even more British than she already was when her emotions were running high only for his smirk to disappear as quickly as it had appeared.

This was normally the part where Americans would debate whether or not to call an ambulance but Alice seemed determined to inflict even more injury to Mark when she slapped at his arm reproachfully. "For God's sake, Mark, are you *trying* to give me a heart attack?" She continued to scold him as, futilely, Mark ducked way from Alice's blows in surprise when suddenly her attack halted and Alice stepped back looking concerned.

Mark watched her carefully, unsure if a second wave of aggression was imminent until Alice turned away from him to take a few deep breaths and Mark relaxed slightly, rubbing his upper arm where she had landed a particularly painful blow. "You really are stupid sometimes, Mark" Alice sighed turning back to him and moving towards him purposefully, making Mark lean back quickly, eyes wide in apprehension. Alice huffed. "I'm *not* going to hit you" She reassured him lifting her hand to steady his head as she lifted herself onto her toes to look at the split on his temple more carefully and slowly Mark felt his smirk return as he came to a realisation.

"You were worried for me" He spoke, looking down at her smugly. Alice glared at him. "I know your name and you're bleeding from your head"

She replied frankly "I'm morally *obliged* to be worried"

"Sure"

"Fuck you"

A moment passed.

"You're still here"

"Fine"

Irritably Alice pulled away, wiping her hand that had some blood on it against his already bloody t - shirt. "Deal with it yourself then" she muttered turning on her heel and beginning to move back towards the nightclub doorway where her friend was stood, speaking to Jay worriedly. "Hey" Mark called after her "Hey, wait" Gently he gripped her wrist and tugged her back to face him.

"I was joking" He backtracked, chuckling quietly "And I don't have any bandages at home so I kind of need your help" Alice raised an eyebrow, looking unamused. "You can buy some on your way" she answered moving to turn again but Mark was faster, taking her wrist again and pulling her back before she had a chance to move. "I'm broke" He responded.

Alice pursed her lips as Mark once again smirked smugly. She glanced at her friend once again before raising her eyebrows in questioning. Evelyn halted her conversation momentarily to wave her hand in a gesture that said "Go on. I'll sort myself out"

Alice sighed in annoyance. "You'll need more than a plaster for that" she spoke reluctantly "I might have some steri-strips at home but my car is down the road- oh sorry. *Block*" Alice rolled her eyes resting her small handbag onto her thigh as she began to rummage through it before pulling out a small tissue from a resealable package and half handing, half throwing it at Mark.

"So, try not to die on the way there"

CHAPTER SEVENTEEN

Alice

ALICE considered asking Mark what had made him leave the club and do what he did as she drove through the night traffic of America's big apple, but somehow she knew it would be futile. A part of her had guessed that even Mark himself wasn't entirely sure and pressing him about it would only confuse him further. She and Mark had both had enough emotionally driven, reckless actions for one night.

So, Alice waited until they were safely behind closed doors before she spoke to him next as she dumped her handbag and coat on the counter pushed up against the wall opposite her front door. It was a tasteful oak wood furnishing that seemed almost out of place amongst the abundance of modern architecture and décor that seemed to make up her Aunt's apartment.

'*A little like Mark and I*' She had thought as she made her way into the kitchen area where the first aid kit was kept. Neither of the youngsters were *really* where they belong. Alice was homesick and overshadowed in the concrete jungle of New York while Mark was lost and wayward. Corrupt almost. Alice just couldn't figure out how.

And in what way.

"Sit down" She instructed him moving into the glossy but neutral kitchen area behind the dining table she had just signalled Mark to sit at. "Mind you don't get blood on the seat though" She added hastily as she pulled a box of first aid supplies from its place in an overhead cupboard located in the corner of the room.

Obediently Mark took a seat, sitting further forwards than normal to keep his bloody shirt a good distance away from the back of the velvet cushioned seat. "You shouldn't have left like that" she said matter-of-factly as she dumped the box on the table in front of him. Immediately Mark was defending himself.

"Says who?" He replied looking amused "I'm allowed to leave when I want to" Alice rolled her eyes. "I'm not saying you shouldn't have left at all" she countered pulling two alcohol wipes and some steri-strips from the now open box. "Just don't leave when you can barely stand by yourself or at least not alone" Mark shut his mouth quickly. Alice could see in his eyes what he was thinking. Was he really that drunk?

To be fair, it probably hadn't felt like it half an hour ago but then again he had also probably been high on adrenaline. Perhaps they cancelled each other out or maybe it had just been too soon for the alcohol to have entered his bloodstream.

All the same, however, Mark swayed backwards proving Alice right and quickly Alice grabbed his shoulders to steady him before picking up one of the antiseptic wipes once again. Moments passed as, gently but firmly, Alice cleaned the now drying out cut in a tense quietness until Mark broke the silence with a hiss of pain. "Don't be such a baby" Alice reprimanded as she dropped the wipe on the table to pick up the other and use it to clean away the blood running down his face and neck.

"Easy for you to say"

"It's just a little alcohol"

"And it *stings*"

Alice huffed, shaking her head as she continued on regardless.

"I wasn't alone" Mark pointed out.

Alice huffed again.

"You might as well have been" she answered, her voice changing from a scolding tone to a more worried one. "I didn't see your friend getting involved until he absolutely had to" Mark scoffed, only for the sound to turn into a second hiss. "He's not my friend" He renounced, grimacing as Alice pulled at the skin of his temple to steri-strip his gaping cut together.

"Then you *were* alone" Alice replied shortly, unwrapping a large plaster to stick it over his newly "stripped" cut for good measure before gathering together all the empty wrappers to take them away. "Why did you leave anyway?" she questioned as she threw the wrappers in the bin concealed in a cupboard underneath the kitchen sink. "Was it because I was there?"

Mark scoffed. "Don't flatter yourself" he replied rudely "It had nothing to do with you. I just didn't like the people I was with" It was partially true. He *didn't* like the people he was with but in that moment; he loathed them and it had *everything* to do with her. Alice frowned, taking two glasses from where they had been drip drying beside the sink for almost two days now and filled them each with cold tap water. "Why were you with them then?" She asked placing one of the two glasses in front of him "If you didn't want to be there, why were you?"

Mark took a moment to take her in more carefully. The distance in the club and the darkness of the alleyway had prevented him from seeing all of her clearly before but now, as she sat under the warm yellow lights hanging above the dining table. Alice sat down opposite him unaware as Mark's eyes followed each curve accentuated by each tight seam on her dress, each sparkle of highlight brushed delicately over her cheekbones and much like a red wine the same colour of her dress, Alice seemed to radiate a new breed of class and sophistication that only she seemed to possess. A uniqueness. A difference.

"You look good in red" Mark complimented ignoring her question in favour of a subject he seemed to find far more fascinating. Alice looked surprised, taken aback by Mark's sudden and unexpected flattery before she smiled and raised an eyebrow. "So do you" she responded sarcastically as she took a sip of water, leaving a faintly red lipstick mark on the rim of her glass. Mark's face took on a confused look as he looked down at his white shirt and dark jeans before glimpsing the blood staining most of his shirt's left shoulder.

He looked back up nodding. "Touché" He answered simply.

"I think my uncle might have left some things from before I moved in" Alice said standing to turn away from the dining table and move towards the modern looking staircase behind them. "Let me see if there's anything that might fit you"

CHAPTER EIGHTEEN

Mark

MARK let out a hum of acknowledgement as he leant back in his seat, watching her disappear up the winding staircase before standing himself and following her footsteps out of the dining area but turning the opposite way to enter the living area.

Mark envied every part of Alice's lifestyle. The education, the opportunities. This apartment. It's clean, modern design. It's tidiness and it's space. The décor and furnishings must cost more than his own small flat alone but it was more what Alice's life *lacked* than what it had. A calm mundaneness and normality. No constant craving for something more, no frenzied searching for something to fill a void somewhere deep inside of her just, contentment.

"Mark?" Alice's voice came from the dining area and quickly Mark turned from the large floor to ceiling windows that overlooked the New York skyline, pulled away abruptly from his thoughts. "Over here" He called, turning back to gaze out at the shimmering skyscrapers as they sparkled with lit up windows in the dark, like Christmas trees after everyone had gone to bed.

Slowly Alice moved away from the dining table to stand beside him and look out the same window. "Everyone can see you" Mark murmured, almost incoherently. Alice looked away from the shining New York skyline to study Mark's face.

Mark didn't move. Just stared straight ahead at his reflection in the glass opposite him. At first glance he seemed completely stoic. His face, like normal, remained expressionless as they stood in near silence but this time there was a hidden emotion under all his enigma. Even Mark wasn't quite sure if it was worry or fear. Perhaps, even, it was a mixture of both, but whichever it was, *whatever* it was, it made Mark uncomfortable.

It worried him that he couldn't conceal his emotions when he was with Alice. Mark knew better than anyone that he, real as he seemed, was nothing more than a tragically flawed character in the story of his life. A classically, cold and distant personality for no reason other than to protect the people around him from the only thing he was *truly* afraid of. But now Alice's own life had merged with his to create a riveting new sub-plot. But like a bridge constructed in two parts that didn't line up or a jigsaw piece forced into the wrong space. Something didn't fit and Mark could see that Alice sensed it too.

Slowly the girl lifted a neatly folded t-shirt and pair of joggers and held it in front of Mark, waiting for him to take them. "*You* can see *everyone*" She replied still watching his face carefully as it flickered with uncertainty and he hesitantly turned to look at her with the same hard, cold stare he had fabricated those two years ago but the concealed emotion remained, only given away when Mark couldn't help but chew on his lip subconsciously. A habit, Mark was sure, Alice would easily recognise as a serial offender herself.

Quickly he stopped.

"Is it that there's no privacy?" she asked quietly as, hesitantly, Mark took the clothes from her. He thought for a moment. He shook his head. "That would mean I'm worried for myself" He answered truthfully, shifting uncomfortably, and looking down at his feet "It's other people I'm worried about" He confessed.

Tightly, Mark gripped the clothes. The worry was crippling. The urge to just spill every one of his darkest secrets then and there was almost unbearable but the consequences were unfathomable. "I'm not normal, Alice" He let out quietly, his whole body rigid now "I don't function in this society and the people around me shouldn't be involved in that" Mark paused. "But now I've involved myself in your life. And I need to get out before I involve you in mine"

Unceremoniously, Mark dropped the clothes on the sofa in front of him and pulled his bloodied shirt over his head, despite Alice's presence beside him. He might have had too much to drink but Mark had spent almost the entirety of the last two years either drunk or dosed up on caffeine and a few beers had never loosened his lips before, so he was going to make god damn sure it wouldn't tonight.

As much as he wanted it to.

"Wha-?"

"Thank you for helping me out back there" Mark interrupted her, replacing his shirt with her uncle's. It hung drearily on Marks lean figure, three sizes too big for him but deftly Mark tucked the front in his, still, somewhat clean jeans before turning quickly to move away from the living area. "But I should leave you alone now"

Alice stood frozen, her lips slightly parted to form a soft 'o' shape as if she wanted to speak but didn't know what to say. A part of Mark wished she did. A part of him desperately wanted her to call him back. A part of him wanted her to see through his every lie and force the truth from his lips.

But she didn't.

She didn't utter a word and instead she remained still and silent as Mark did his best to march on in a straight line, only his pride stopping him from turning back completely. Mark grimaced as he resisted the urge to look back when he reached the front door but even the little pride he had left couldn't stop him from hesitating as he gripped the door handle.

It wasn't long. No more than a second. But it was enough time for Alice to call out. It was her chance to stop him or try to. But she made the right decision. She didn't take her chance. She stayed quiet and Mark took *his* chance to walk out of her apartment, and her life. Forever.

CHAPTER NINETEEN

Alice

MARK was right.

Nothing about his story was normal.

There was too much missing. Too many holes for it to all add up. And Mark knew it. Mark knew himself like he was the very author who had penned his character. But he seemed determined to stop anyone else knowing him in that way. He seemed determined to conceal as much as he possibly could. He knew more about Alice now than she would even get the chance to learn of him and a part of her felt angry, betrayed almost, that she had been so open with him only to receive nothing in return. But another, much more rational, part of Alice knew it wasn't his fault.

Once again Mark gave her nothing. No signs, no tells and even less information. But no matter how little she knew. No matter how confused he made her. Alice knew one thing at least. Mark was anxious. He was afraid that he would slip up or that he would let something on he shouldn't. Or couldn't. He still had his story to tell. But something had sewn his mouth shut and Alice wanted to know what and more importantly how to remove it. Because just like in the night club, where his dark demeanour had drawn her in, this layer of Mark only made the attraction she felt to him ten times stronger.

Alice, herself, couldn't face the idea of going back to the way it was before him. The normality, the mundane rotation of the same routine over and over again. Mark had given her a taste of spontaneity. He had planted the seed of doubt in her tedious cycle that triggered her to finally *do* something and no matter how much danger or tribulation he brought with him.

She wanted more.

She wanted more and she wanted *him*.

His teasing. His coldness and his enigma. She wanted all of it because she would crack it. She would break the code that was Mark Liu. She would force her way into his life the way he had broken into hers and maybe. Just maybe. One day she would overtake him in his game of mystery and she would be one step ahead of him. It would be *him* chasing after *her*. And not the other way around. Like it was now, as Alice forced her legs to move. Hurrying out of the apartment and into the hallway Mark had long since passed though.

She wasn't sure how far he would have been able to get as she left the apartment but she was relieved when she was able to catch sight of the bright white shirt he wore just as he disappeared into the elevator. Stumbling in her impractical high heels Alice, desperately, ran down the hallway as Mark turned to face the closing doors of the elevator and shocked, Mark's eyes widened moments before the two doors met.

Seconds too late Alice hurtled into the two barricades before slapping the cold metal in frustration and pushing herself away from the machine to turn towards the stairwell doorway. Of course, the stupid thing would be up and working as soon as she *needed* it to malfunction. Not only did she have no idea how close to the ground floor Mark was, now *she* was very unlikely to make it there herself. Unlikely to make it there *alive* in any case.

Finally giving in, Alice risked pausing at the next floor landing to yank the sharp, aggressive looking shoes from her feet and fling them into the wall beside her. She abandoned them, running much more effectively down the remaining stairs and in the absence of such debilitating footwear, it wasn't long before Alice had reached the ground floor.

Immediately she was able to locate Mark in the near empty lobby of the residential building. He moved hastily and carelessly, almost walking into a surprised looking doorman as he headed for the exit. "Mark!" Alice called out, rushing across the lobby to catch up to him "Mark wait!"

Abruptly he stopped, stumbling slightly at the sudden change of speed, still drunk. Mark's shoulders rose and fell dramatically as if he had just let out an annoyed sigh, or a relieved one, but nevertheless he remained still as Alice hurried to stop just behind him. A moment of tense silence passed as they both stood facing the doorway and Alice stared at Mark's back, all the things she was about to say forgotten.

"Where are you going?" She croaked, chest heaving as she tried to catch her breath. Mark turned his head to the side and Alice felt her brows furrow as she registered the hard look on his face.

"Where do you think?" he replied shortly "Home"

"You'll never get there, the state you're in"

 "I've done it before"

 "And I won't let you do it again, it's dangerous" Slowly Alice's confidence crept back as her worry for Mark's safety overruled her concern for his perception of her.

 "You seemed happy to let me go in that alleyway"

 "That's different. That was before I realised…" Alice cut herself off and suddenly Mark's hard expression fell as he turned to face her fully now, waiting for her to finish. "Before I realised that you were right" Mark looked dubious as he watched her but still made no move to continue out into the city streets. "About what?" he asked

 "About everything" Alice responded gulping when her mouth suddenly felt bone dry "You're not normal" She paused considering her next words carefully "And you *have* burst into my life like ten tons of dynamite exploding all at the same time. You're annoying and rude and unnecessarily cold but you always seem to have a solution to everyone's problems apart from your own despite appearing to be fully aware of them, which *baffles* me. You can read me like a book but you never let me know *anything* about you and yet you were right *again* in that alleyway-"

Alice stopped short again when unexpectedly Mark moved. Not towards the doorway like she expected, but instead towards her, not stopping until their bodies were only millimetres apart.

"That even though I don't know anything about you" She continued, softly now "And I feel like I'm banging my head against a brick wall over and over again when I'm with you" Alice took a deep breath as Mark leant down, as if he couldn't hear her properly now that she was speaking so quietly. "I *do* care about you"

Gently their noses brushed against each other.

"And not just because I know your name"

CHAPTER TWENTY

Mark

MARK wasn't surprised when Alice confessed that she cared for him.

Like she had said, he could read the girl like a book. What surprised Mark, was that anyone *at all* could find it in themselves to care for him when, up until now, he had managed to keep everyone he came into contact with a safe distance away from him and his secrets.

But Alice wasn't just anyone. At least, not anymore.

Alice was unlike any other person he had come across in New York. He couldn't just ignore her. It was impossible for him to disassociate from her like he could so easily with his friends. Alice had become his new drink, ten times more potent than the alcohol and caffeine he pumped himself full of. His own personal brand of adrenaline, one hundred times more exhilarating than the rush of fighting. And one hundred thousand times more addicting.

Mark squeezed his eyes shut when that familiar feeling of desperate need overtook him. From where he stood he could feel Alice's warmth radiate through the air to his own body and if he took half a step closer that gap would be closed. Once more though, he hesitated. He knew what he was about to do was wrong but the last of his endurance had been spent on his last show of self-discipline and his resistance had been worn thin.

Mark gave in.

For the second time that night, Mark surrendered himself to his most basic of instincts and he did something he had been wanting to do since they had spent the entire night in that coffee shop together.

He kissed her.

Softly and passionately and completely unexpectedly Mark pressed his lips against hers and in an instant his entire being was alight with two-years-worth of pent up feelings and emotions burning him from the inside out.

It was thrilling. And petrifying. And the *very* rush Mark had been seeking all his life

Right now, as their kiss deepened and their bodies pressed against each other. Mark too came to a realisation. That he didn't know himself as well as *either* of them had thought, because for all he had finally come to understand now, in this very moment. It had still taken him this long to see, that *he* had come to care for Alice, as much as she cared for him.

And it was exactly that, that would destroy them both.

PART TWO

CHAPTER TWENTY-ONE

Alice

WINTER had arrived in New York, along with the month of November, in a series of damp, dreary days, during which the sky was overcast with grey foreboding clouds. Over the course of these days, work had become a foreign concept to Alice as her time was split between chasing what appeared to be thin air with her, still, unfruitful investigations and spending more and more time with Mark.

Nothing much actually changed the night after they had kissed in the foyer of Alice's apartment building. Mark was still an enigma. A strange amalgamation of jigsaw puzzle and riddle. Alice still remained overloaded with work and not enough time to do it. That following night, though, Mark was waiting for her. Leaning against his shiny, black Vauxhall in front of the building's car park entrance as she turned in. And this time, instead of wearing his usual, angry expression on his face like he always did, Mark smiled as Alice stopped her car beside him and leant out the open window.

"What are you doing here?" she asked smiling back when Mark moved to lean against the top of the car as he spoke. "What?" He replied raising his eyebrows in fake surprise "Are you not pleased to see me? Would you like me to go back to the hole I crawled out of?" Quickly he stepped back holding his arms up in surrender as he moved towards his own vehicle slowly.

"No, wait!" Alice had laughed before Mark could take another step back "Come back, you dork. I just meant you don't usually wait for me to get home outside my building" Again Mark let his elbow rest on her MINI's rooftop having walked the short distance back to the small car.

"What's changed?" she rephrased.

Mark's smile widened.

"I just thought you might want to go and get some coffee" he replied.

That was Mark's turning point. And Alice's somewhat. Because that moment was the first time Alice had ever been able to read Mark. That night, Mark wasn't asking if she wanted to go to the coffee shop over the road. He was *telling* her that *he* wanted to and that night, for the first time. Mark answered Alice when she asked him something about himself. He told her how the first night they had spent in that coffee shop was not the first time he had struggled to sleep. That he had spent so many sleepless nights here that, Giovanni the shop owner, had practically offered him the night-time shift and Alice surprised him in return. When she admitted she struggled to sleep also.

Since then, Mark and Alice's relationship had grown from just chance encounters. Now, night after night was spent in what had become "their" coffee shop, sitting in the dimly lit space talking about whatever it was on their minds, or rather, Alice's. Gradually as Alice spent more and more time with Mark in this new, comfortable setting, she realised that Mark wasn't shut out to the world the way she thought he was. He was attentive and a good listener and no less human than the next person. It just took a little more effort to get him to open up.

Even now as he allowed her to understand certain parts of him, Alice could see that Mark was still concealing other parts. Parts she wasn't sure he would ever let her see. But for now Alice was just pleased that their "relationship" no longer felt so one sided. Mark was engaging in his own way. Making an effort, so to speak.

Whilst Alice had made a lot of progress socially, however, her continuing investigations into the recent murder in Washington Square Park had almost completely grinded to a halt. Day after day passed and Alice was still no closer to tracking down the culprit. By the end of the month she was ready to throw the towel in as she scoured newspaper clippings and old yearbooks looking for some clue as to who the girl was but no matter how hard she tried. How closely she scrutinised each and every scrap of paper she could get her hands on. Alice found no leads. No information. Not even a singular forename.

Until one day a group of three rowdy boys entered the NYU Bobst library in a calamity of thuds followed by excited and jeering shouts.

"Oi, Robin mate! Come on!" Another distinctly British sounding voice came from the entrance.

Surprised at hearing the familiar clear cut accent, Alice looked up from her messy library table to see what the disruption had been about.

At the entrance two boys stood over another as he clumsily collected a pile of books he had clearly just knocked over. One of the two above him, younger looking than the others, was shaking his head in disapproval, making his grown out, dark blonde hair fall from the top of his head to rest just above his brow bone. Carelessly he pushed it back up to the top of his head and out of the way as he nudged a book near his rugged black converse towards the boy below him.

"Just because you two have graduated doesn't mean you get to treat the place like shit" He told him wandering away from the group and looking around, searching for something as the boy beside him held back, laughing hysterically at his friends misfortune.

"Since when do you care about the crap in this place?" he retorted, making no effort to help his other friend finally hoist the books back onto the shelf unit beside the entrance. Quickly he pushed the pile back as it threatened to topple over the side again and let out a sigh of relief when he managed to stabilize it against the wall behind. The boy ahead of the other two laughed. "I don't" he answered simply "But it's me who gets the blame if someone finds out. You guys aren't meant to be here right now, remember?"

Behind him his friends exchanged a glance with one another. The darker haired of the two, the one who had knocked the books over, shrugged, making the leather jacket he was wearing squeak as he moved before they started jogging to catch up to the younger of the group. "What did you say you had to do here again?" The other of the two left behind asked. This one was more tanned, although granted it was fading with the lack of sun as of recent and he had shorter hair than the youngest of the three. It was only visible from the small fringe that pushed through from under the grey beanie pulled carelessly onto the back of his head, like the hat had been a last minute after thought as he left the house. It matched the t shirt he wore under a blue denim jacket and concealed most of his head to stay in place but if Alice craned her neck just enough, she was able to catch a glimpse of the same dark blonde coloured hair the youngest had when he turned his head to glance back at the pile of books they had left behind.

"I didn't" The youngest responded pulling a book from the section almost directly opposite Alice's position marked; *Journalism*. "All you need to know is, I can't find what I'm looking for" he elaborated. Sighing in frustration the boy slammed the book back into its place, having glanced at it for a grand total of ten seconds.

Alice watched in both amusement and curiosity. None of the boys looked as if they spent much time in libraries and judging by their hopelessly careless behaviour this was one of a very small number of visits for them all. The youngest, however, despite the fact that he clearly did *not* spend a lot of time in the aisles of the same building Alice almost inhabited, seemed strangely familiar and it was this strange feeling that prompted Alice to do something she never normally would have done otherwise.

"W-what is it you're looking for?" She spoke across to them from where she was sat. Quickly the group looked up towards the end of the aisle before turning to scan the small study space tucked away between the bookshelves at the end of the room. It didn't take long for their gazes to fall on Alice, especially when she was the only one of the very few people in the room even looking at them but for a moment, Alice thought they might ignore her. Turn back to whatever it was they were doing now that they had found out where the voice had come from. Much to her relief, though, Dark Blonde the younger, smiled, pushing a half pulled out book back onto the shelf so he could step away and move towards the table Alice was seated at smoothly.

"The first draft of my journalism thesis is due next week" The boy spoke. He smirked. "I figured I should probably *start* it by then at least"

Alice tried not to let her shock show. It was none of her business how her classmates chose to conduct themselves but the very idea of not even *starting* an essay as important as her *thesis* might well have sent her into a seizure had it been *her* in his predicament. The fact that this boy seemed completely unworried by the dire situation he was in was extraordinary considering it could decide if he continued on into his second year at the university.

A part of Alice wanted to query his horrendous lateness, half convinced that there must be an equally extraordinary reason behind it all but, instead, she locked in on something else that he had said.

"You're studying Journalism too?" she asked putting down her pen to give him her undivided attention now. Dark Blonde nodded leaning forwards on the chair opposite her to peer over her work. "And Photography" he added "Journalism was kind of an after-thought" he explained. Alice's mouth opened ever so slightly to form a soft 'o' shape with her lips. "I *knew* I recognised you from somewhere!" She exclaimed "I'm studying Journalism too. I saw you in our first class with Professor Darcy and then you never came again. I always thought you had dropped out of the course"

Alice cringed, only realising until after she had said it how rude her remark had sounded but much to her relief the boy in front of her chuckled, nodding slowly as he glanced back at his two friends approaching from where they had been stood previously. "Sounds like something I'd do" he replied nonchalantly, pulling the folder Alice had laid open in front of her towards his side of the table, his eyes darting from side to side as he scanned the document quickly. "Is this your thesis?" he asked lifting one of the pages to look at the rest of the contents of the tattered, brown file.

Quickly Alice clawed the pages back to her side of the table. "N-no" she stammered closing the file hastily "T-this is just..." Alice cut herself off as she looked up at the boy and saw his shocked face. Eyes wide and skin pasty white as he reached toward the file again. "L-let me see that photo" he murmured. Alice laid her hand over the folder defensively. "I-I'm not sure..." Alice started.

"I'm not sure that's a good idea" she was going to say. But before she uttered those last four words the boy had interrupted her. And those four words were immediately forgotten as he lowered himself into the chair he had been leaning on. Again he reached out to the papers, waiting for her to hand him that one glossy photograph.

"I know her" he whispered.

CHAPTER TWENTY-TWO

Mark

MARK had never regretted an action more than he regretted kissing Alice.

He wouldn't have changed it for the world.

He would have kissed her over and over again until the guilt caused him to explode if it was even possible to replay that moment as many times as he so desperately wanted to. Mark thought he might let it play on loop for infinity if he could but love it as he did and yearn for it as he might, he had opened a can of worms now. A can of ravenous, rabid, man eating worms with sharp teeth and poisoned skin and a bigger appetite than his head.

Which was pretty big.

Mark *was* selfish but Mark, this time, had committed the *ultimate* act of selfishness. Because when he finally allowed himself to take what he wanted from Alice, it wasn't that he had taken it forcibly. It wasn't even that Mark had taken with every intention to continue taking. It was that he had taken that warmth, that intimacy from Alice. Knowing full well that he, in that act, however indirectly – or directly, had been the one to pull the trigger on her life as she knew it.

There was a chance that moment had happened earlier. Perhaps it had been the day he had helped her find her keys to prove a point or the night he had sat opposite her in "their" coffee shop. Either way, though, that split second it took to let go of all the restraints he had tied himself into, was the moment he knew it for sure. The moment he acknowledged that no matter how much he cared for her. No matter how much he wanted to keep her life the stable equilibrium it was. His selfish wants would always prevail and eventually, one way or another, he would somehow destroy her.

Trespass in her life, like he had trespassed on all the private land in New York City. Vandalise it like he had graffitied on all the trains he had been able to find and hurt her worse than the many people he had hurt in the last two years. But if the last two years had taught him anything. It was don't try to delay the inevitable. Because the inevitable always found a way of happening. Mark knew that better than anyone.

All the same he hadn't expected the fall from grace to begin so quickly.

The first sign was when Alice had called him earlier than normal. Mark had given her his number when one night he had been running late.

Over the past month he and Alice had settled into a comfortable routine and each night Mark stood, waiting at the entrance of the same underground parking area until one night a job taking longer than normal had caused Mark to arrive at Alice's apartment building nearly two hours later than he usually did. Alice had been so worried at his mysterious disappearance that when he finally arrived at the dark faux wood of her front door he had barely completed a single knock before she had frantically thrown it open.

It had been the first time they had realised that, despite being in *"an age of communication"* neither of the pair had any means of *communicating* with the other until they were face to face. Mark had hesitated to give her any traceable evidence to link her to him at first but seeing how worked up she had got herself had made up his mind. He was already seeing her in person. What was one more form of communication?

Since then they had formed a new routine. One that consisted of daily phone calls to check if he was coming to "their" coffee shop that night, to which the answer was always "yes" They both knew it was just another excuse to speak to one another, though, just like the phone call *Mark* made each night to make sure she had got home safely was an excuse to speak to her even further into the early morning after they had left "their coffee shop"

Today, however, Alice had phoned him nearly one and a half hours before she normally left the NYU library Mark had first met her outside and he had been so surprised that he had double checked the time on his car dashboard when her call had lit up his phone screen.

Three o'clock.

Normally, Alice didn't call until at least five o'clock once she had finished working for the day and the sudden break from normality made Mark do something he hadn't done since he lost his friend and his father all in one night. Mark panicked.

What if Alice's mysterious phone call was actually a call for help? What if she had been hurt? What if it was already too late? The very thought made Mark fumble to answer the phone so carelessly that the already battered device almost went flying out of his hand as he raised it to his ear. "Alice?" He spoke.

"Mark!" Alice's voice rang out from the phone speaker "Mark, you have *no idea* what's just happened!" She exclaimed. Quickly Mark lifted his other hand to grip the steering wheel in front of him "What, Alice?" Mark questioned franticly "What happened? Where are you? Are you ok? Are you hurt?"

"W-what?" Alice answered sounding confused before, unexpectedly, quiet chuckling came from the other end of the line "Mark, I'm *fine*. What did you think had happened?" she asked. Mark closed his eyes and leaned forwards to rest his forehead against the wheel he still had in a vice like grip. Slowly, he took a deep breath in an attempt to slow his racing heart. She was ok. She was speaking to him. She was fine.

"Nothing" He replied, desperately trying hide the worry he had let slip "I didn't think anything had happened" If the worry had made him feel uncomfortable, it had nothing on the embarrassment he felt afterwards. Mark could just see the cogs in Alice's pretty little mind, she would be thrilled he had expressed anything other than discontentment. Even if the expression had been completely unwarranted melodrama.

"You thought I was in trouble, didn't you?" Alice deduced. He could practically hear the smile in her voice "You were *worried* for me, weren't you?" Mark rolled his eyes and lifted his head. Despite all her clumsiness and inefficiency the girl could most certainly *remember*. "Ha. Ha." Mark answered quite obviously unamused "Very funny. Hilarious. Hysterical, in fact. Absolutely side-splitting…"

"Ok, ok" Alice interrupted almost splitting her own sides with uncontrollable laughter "You'd better stop before you run out of words" Mark smiled ever so slightly. "I already have" he confessed, releasing his grip on the steering wheel a little so that he could slide his hand along the curve to the bottom of the perfect circle "What was it you were going to say?" He asked pulling the conversation back to what it had started with. They could be there for hours talking about nothing and everything but Mark still had two more hours before he finished work and fifteen minutes to get to his next job.

"Oh! Yeah of course!" Alice spoke excitedly "It's about the case" She explained. The sound of a car door being shut interrupted her for a second followed by books, no doubt, being chucked onto the passenger seat of Alice's MINI. "I know who the girl is"

Mark's stomach lurched.

"Y-you do?" He croaked, his mouth suddenly bone dry. Alice hummed in response. "Her name is Abigail Wilson and she's been working in local night clubs as an exotic dancer since she was eighteen. That's why I haven't been able to find her in any college yearbooks. She never went to one" Alice paused as papers shuffled in the background. "There's a guy in my Journalism class who says he and his friends know her." She went on, papers still shuffling "They used to see her in clubs all the time and *he* says that her mother lives close by in…" Again Alice paused the shuffling growing louder and, by the sound of it, more frustrated.

Suddenly Alice let out a cry of triumph. "Rutgers Street" She announced "Rutgers Street near Manhattan Bridge. I was thinking you and I could go and visit her…"

"Wait, wait, wait" Mark interjected suddenly when he had finally managed to process all the information Alice had just thrown at him "W-who is this guy? How did he even know you were investigating this gir-... *Abigail*" Even saying her name out loud felt strange, like he was disrespecting her dead memory in some way.

"Oh" Alice replied brightly "He came into the library while I was looking through some old newspapers trying to find a lead. He seemed pretty shaken when he saw the photo, poor thing, but he gave me his number so I could ask him anything else if I needed to bless him" Mark's head hurt as his mind reeled with Alice's new development. "And this guy's in your Journalism class?" He questioned. More books being dumped somewhere came from the other side of the line. "Yeah" Alice answered, "Actually I didn't realise until right then because he only came to the first class of the year and then kind of disappeared" She went on obliviously "*And* he's British too" she added. Mark froze, realisation dawning on him. "He said his name was Christopher but his friends all call him..."

"Kit" Mark finished for her.

A moment passed and a tense silence fell over the pair when neither Mark nor Alice dared to speak until Mark's voice broke through the stillness. "Alice I'm not sure about this anymore" He let out quietly. It was ok at the start, at the start it was just him and her but now the two parts of his life had overlapped. It was exactly what Mark had been trying to avoid. Keeping Alice away from his "friends" would be impossible now, no matter how hard he tried to shield her from them they would find a way to ruin her and there would be nothing he could do to stop them.

"I know Kit and you really don't want to get involved with him and his friends" Mark tried to explain. "He seemed ok to me…" Alice objected innocently. "Well he's not" Mark told her shortly "He's nothing but trouble and his friends are even worse than him. You said yourself, he went to your first class and then disappeared. Doesn't exactly sound like a model student, does it?"

"Wha-…Why have you suddenly changed your mind about this?" Alice asked, sounding irked at Mark's sudden switch "This was your idea"

"I didn't think it would go *this* far" Mark answered thoughtlessly, raising his free hand to run it through his outgrown hair anxiously. "Go how far!?" Alice retorted "Why won't you ever tell me anything? Why is there always something missing?"

"I'm *trying* to protect you!"

"From *what*!?" Alice shouted "*Wake up*, Mark! This is *real* life! Boyfriends don't protect their girlfriends by keeping them in the dark all the time!"

Mark tensed.

Suddenly everything came to an abrupt stop. Like when you slam on the brakes in a car. And in that moment Mark *really* regretted kissing Alice. He cursed himself for being so stupid. For letting it go too far. For letting it *all* go too far. He had thought the night in the club had been too close for comfort and now here he was. Watching Alice make all the wrong friends knowing it was all his fault. Mark had thought he had run out of self-control but the shock of Alice becoming so involved with his friends so quickly had given him an unexpected power surge of fear.

Mark gulped.

If there was one thing more powerful than anger.

It was fear.

"Is that what I am to you?" He asked, his voice barely above a whisper "Your boyfriend?" No sound came from Alice's side of the line until she let out a small sound, as if she was about to say something then stopped just before she got the words out.

"I-I just th-thought that because o-of those nights in the coffee shop a-and the phone calls and the *kiss*…" Alice paused, the anger in her voice coming dangerously close to changing into sadness "Well, what else can you be?"

"Alice" Mark drew out "I can't be your boyfriend" He sighed rubbing his face in frustration "It's complicated but…" Mark cut himself off when he realised even Alice's breathing had fallen silent. "A-Alice?" He spoke.

Again an uncomfortable silence had fallen over them and for a moment Mark thought Alice might have hung up on him when suddenly a crackling told him that Alice was still there.

"You're a real ass hole, Mark. You know that?"

CHAPTER TWENTY-THREE

Alice

ALICE had promised herself that she would use Saturday this week to catch up on school work she had neglected in favour of her investigation. No matter how hard she tried to focus on the words in her textbook, though, or the next sentence she needed to write for her thesis, all she could think of was that phone call with Mark two days before.

Despite being nearly forty eight hours ago now, even the thought of it still made Alice's cheeks burn in humiliation. It made her cringe randomly when she wasn't expecting the mortifying memories to penetrate her thoughts. It gave her a horrid sick feeling in her abdomen like she had been punched in the stomach. Hard. She cursed herself for being so silly as to think that Mark might have willing settled into a relationship like the one she had thought they had.

Of course he wouldn't have committed himself in that way. Of course he wouldn't change like that. Not in the time that they had known each other anyway. Alice wasn't just angry with Mark, though, more than anything else she was angry with herself. For being so stupid. For not realising that Mark wasn't ready and making a fool of herself in the process.

She had spent nearly five hours alternating between overthinking every tiny detail that led up to her explosion of humiliation and hopelessly trying to get something worthwhile done until she finally gave in. Working was impossible with Mark's words and her actions perpetually running through her mind. So huffing disappointedly Alice closed her laptop and stood to walk away from her Aunt's dining table.

Leaving the mountains of papers and books behind her Alice headed into the lounge area of her Aunt's apartment to scoop up the television remote from where it had been discarded carelessly on the cushions of the sofa the last time it had been used and flick on the screen hanging on the far wall.

Immediately the dim apartment was lit up as light streamed across the open space from the machine and Alice squinted as her eyes adjusted to the new light and she fell onto the settee behind her gracelessly already flicking through the channels. Alice was met with endless streams of late night chat shows and reruns of old shows that had probably been played the night before and was about to give up when she passed over one channel playing an out of the ordinary news stream.

Quickly she flicked back to the stream and immediately a young, suited woman in her mid-twenties filled the screen, a grim expression on her face as she looked into the room. She was a pretty lady with the same dark hair as Alice but unlike Alice she possessed the same honey-like complexion as Mark. Alice cringed.

It seemed most things reminded her of Mark but is she was being totally honest with herself, which as of recent, she had not. It was fairly apparent that Mark, currently, was the *only* thing Alice thought of.

"The victim was found early this morning after being left in a nearby alleyway to a club he was known for visiting often and is the most recent of a string of killings that have happened in the Manhattan area thought to be carried out by the same perpetrator due to certain similarities such as timings and close proximity to various clubs in the area between the otherwise separate incidents" The anchor read out loud in that same monotone voice every news reader spoke with.

Alice had always thought that the way news readers delivered their news made it seem so much more dire. For a time she suspected that even something that was meant to be happy and exciting could have been ruined by simply being announced in the same way but this time Alice was filled with an almost inappropriate amount of excitement at hearing that another murder had been committed.

"My name is Angelique Hudson and this was the News at midnight. I'll leave you with Hannah Barnes who has the coming week's weather but from me. It's a good night and goodbye. Thanks for watching"

'Angelique' nodded towards the camera smiling sweetly now that her job was done and turning in her chair before the screen cut to a slim, bleach blonde lady stood in front of a large green screen map talking about belts of low and high pressure. Alice wasn't paying attention, however, already snatching up her mobile phone before hesitating. Calling Mark like she had intended couldn't be an option. Not after their last phone call.

Alice swiped past his name back up to the names beginning with L, then K until she found Kit's name. Tucked between Kiera and Luke, a boy Alice had gone to school with before moving away from Britain but had not once made contact with since leaving, Kit's name burnt into her mind as it stared up at her.

Something felt uncomfortable about calling him. Perhaps it was Mark's insistent warning of him and his unreliability. Almost like she was double crossing him. But Mark had made it clear that there was nothing between them that would make something like this a problem of any sort.

She tapped the phone icon beside it and lifted it to her ear. She had no allegiance or loyalty. If she wanted to call Kit. She would.

CHAPTER TWENTY-FOUR

Mark

 MARK hated clubs.

 But Mark hated this club in particular because The Black Tiger Club was a bad omen. Or perhaps he was the bad omen and The Black Tiger just happened to be the closest thing to blame but it seemed to Mark that whenever something bad happened it was always somehow linked to The Black Tiger. Meeting Jay and Eli. His first deal. Jacob's death. His first fight. Dragging Alice into his world of *mess*. His *last* fight.

It was all one big blood bath after the next but Mark wasn't going to say no to his usual excuse to drink himself blind when Robin had called him to tell him that he and the other boys were going to be at The Black Tiger like usual. Mark didn't *need* any more alcohol. In all honesty if he drank anymore it might be the drink that killed him after the amount of liquor Mark had thrown down himself in the past week.

Mark hadn't realised how much his habits had changed since meeting Alice. Spending so much time with her, he just didn't have the time to be drinking and getting drunk the way he had before. In her absence, though, he had spent most of his time either blindingly drunk or wallowing in self-pity in his and Alice's coffeeshop as he tried to sober up enough to get home without killing himself each night.

Tonight, however, he had finally decided that it didn't matter anymore. Tonight Mark would drink enough to erase any memory of Alice he possessed and then, maybe, the want would go away by itself. Then, maybe, he wouldn't miss her so unbelievably painfully but Mark hadn't considered who else was going to be there.

So, Mark had spent most of the night nursing a rancid bottle of beer and scowling across the table at a completely oblivious Kit who had been drinking the same stuff at double the speed. He had been glassy eyed for the past hour and Mark had half a mind to let his emotions rule him in the absence of alcohol to distract from the almost irrepressible urge to knock Kit right in his oh-so-charming face.

His mind was made whole when Kit's lips became a little too loose not much later, however.

"She was one of those cute secretary types you know?" He shouted over the music "You saw her, Sam" He added nudging the only *slightly* more sober boy next to him. Sam looked up from his drink a surprised expression on his face at being called upon so suddenly. "Adorable little thing wasn't she?" Kit prompted "That Alice girl"

Mark's eyes widened as Sam nodded vigorously in agreement. "Yeah, yeah" He responded, "She had these *massive* glasses on" He spoke up now he knew what the conversation was about. He chuckled. "*Way* too big for her but it looked good" Sam shrugged "I mean, *I'd* lay her" Mark's jaw tensed. "I'm nearly there" Kit answered grinning proudly as he lifted his phone up from the table top "Been talking to her all week" he told them all "I reckon I'll get her in bed by Fri…"

Mark was on his feet before his mind had a chance to register what his body was doing. A moment of shock passed as Kit stopped talking suddenly and the rest of the boys with them looked up at Mark in surprise. Then he was walking away. Out the doors of the club. Left onto the street.

Anywhere that was *away* from Kit. From *them*. He wanted nothing to do with them anymore. He wanted to remove them from his life entirely. Catapult himself back two years in time to before everything went bad. He wished he could have Alice. He wished he could go and sit in "their" coffee shop with her opposite him and talk to her without doing any more damage to her life than he had already.

Mark slowed.

He had damaged her life already. Permanently. Irrevocably. *Irreversibly*. He had *already* ruined her. There was no point in worrying about something happening when it had already happened. All those times Mark had given in. Realised that he could no longer resist her and he would have to accept that someday he would finally mess up her life like his had been. He hadn't realised it had already happened. That the damage was done. And there was nothing he could do now to change that. So why try?

Mark stopped.

And turned around.

CHAPTER TWENTY-FIVE

Alice

ALICE had missed him.

She wanted nothing more than to snatch up her phone and dial his number in the hopes that he might even pick up half as fast as he normally would but every time the urge rose up in her Alice forced herself to be reminded exactly why she was cutting him off. That she should have known better than to think Mark might have opened himself up to her that much.

She realised now, she had been optimistic from the very start of their "relationship" but what

Mark had done the day she had called him, , after much more careful consideration and much more not-so-careful over thinking, had only proved to her that he, despite all the things he had done to convince her otherwise, had not changed one bit.

He was still secretive. He was still confusing and confused. He still spoke in riddles Alice couldn't hope to understand but above all. There was still some part of him, Alice wasn't quite sure where or how or why, but inevitably there *was* a part of him that *enjoyed* the distress he put her in. She was sure of it. Why else would he push her so out of her comfort zone over and over again? Then try to leave her to fend for herself when she needed him most? It was a never ending cycle of change, adaption and then more change.

But just like she had broken her last monotonous routine from before she met Mark, Alice was determined to break this much more corrosive pattern. The only problem was, last time Alice had, had Mark to help her. This time Mark was the very thing that was making it almost impossible.

Over the course of the week that followed, Alice had begun to understand why Mark hated windows so much. Each night, at the same time, Mark stood on the sidewalk outside their coffee shop. Each night her phone rang and each night

Alice ignored the call, knowing it would be from him but never once did the thought cross her mind to block him.

Alice knew that Mark couldn't see her from where she was stood in her apartment but there was something about the way he looked up at her building, his expression uncharacteristically pained instead of his normal stoic, that made it feel like his eyes were piercing straight through her very being. Alice tried hard to ignore the pull dragging her towards the very man who had turned her life into an even bigger mess than it already was but no matter what she did to try and distract herself, she always found herself glancing down at that coffee shop just to see if he was still there.

On Friday night, ashamed as she was, Alice had been waiting for Mark to arrive at their coffee shop. She had been disappointed, however, when the glossy black Corsa that Mark drove never pulled into the parking bay just outside the building opposite hers. Alice hadn't even received a phone call like she normally did at this time and although this silence, this alone-ness, had been exactly what Alice had been wishing for since the day she had been so harshly rejected by Mark. Alice found herself wishing even more that she could turn back time and do it all again.

No matter how hard she tried to forget about him as soon as she had been granted her wish Mark was the only thing that filled her mind. Even as she stared endlessly at the collage of photographs and news clippings she had created against her dining room wall, she realised that answers seemed to come much more easily when Mark was in her life. No matter how frustrating that may be.

All week Alice had been in a furious pursuit of more and more new information and rapidly the small gallery she had created from the papers in her case file had grown to occupy almost the entire area of the wall between her kitchen and the large window opposite it. With the combined effort of her and Kit the pair had managed to uncover a second murder in the area. This time a bartender from the same club Abigail worked at, about two weeks prior to Abigail's own death.

The man, Jethro Garcia, had come from a deprived area in Manhattan similar to Abigail and was known for using his location in a downtown bar as a way to augment his measly earnings selling easy drugs to customers in the club. Kit had said that he and his friends knew of him but had never bought any. Something about the way he had said *'They didn't need to'*, however, made

Alice suspect that it was one of the reasons Mark had warned her off him.

All the same, Kit was proving invaluable to Alice's research. Foreign as he was to New York, Kit seemed to know the city better than even the people Alice had met, who had spent their entire lives there. The difference was, Kit knew all the hidden details most people overlooked, the dark backstreets and hidden nooks that only a contumacious boy like Kit *would* know and Alice *needed* to.

One large map hung on her wall among the various photos and news articles she had collected and on it key locations were marked with brightly coloured circular stickers like tiny little beacons gripping your attention. No matter how many strands of red ribbon pinned up or colourful stickers Alice placed carefully on her cheap corner store map, though, she was still no closer to finding a trend.

Alice was close to giving up for the night and going to bed when all of sudden her attention was drawn from her makeshift gallery to her phone on the dining table beside her as it lit up to signal an incoming phone call. For a moment Alice thought it might have been Mark. That he just happened to be running late tonight and if she looked down now she would see his silhouette moving in the dim coffee shop below but as she quickly snatched up the device her heart sunk when she realised the number calling her was not saved in her phone.

Alice hesitated. Ever since Alice had first been entrusted a phone by her parents she had been warned about the dangers of picking up to unsaved numbers. *"It could be a cold caller"* and *"It's probably someone just trying to sell you something"* echoed in her mind as her thumb hovered over the screen until finally she dragged her thumb up the delicate glass to answer the call.

Alice wasn't sure if it was possible for her heart to sink further than it had earlier and jump straight to her throat all at the same time but when Mark's voice came from her phone speaker it had felt like her entire body had entered a spasm of excitement and anger.

"Alice…"

"I thought I made it very clear to you that I didn't want any more contact with you, Mark" Alice interrupted him. She couldn't let him speak. If she did he would do that thing with her. He would somehow make her see everything in a different way. A way that put him in the clear and her in the wrong and Alice had, had enough of being manipulated.

"I know Alice..." Mark started

"I thought me not picking up your calls would be enough of a clue but you really are something else, Mark" Alice cut him off angrily "Using someone else's phone to trick me into picking up the..."

"No that's not it..." Mark tried to interject

"Save it" Alice snapped "I don't want to hear it and when I hang up this..."

"Wait! Wait, wait, wait!" Mark exclaimed suddenly.

Alice froze, her phone half lowered half raised so that all she could hear was Mark's small tinny voice drifting through the air from her phone speaker to her ear. "Don't hang up" Mark let out "I-I only have one phone call" He stammered. A moment passed as Alice processed what Mark said before, slowly, Alice pressed the phone back to her ear. "O-only one?" She repeated, confused "Why only one pho- Mark have you been *arrested*!?" Alice exclaimed.

There was a moment's hesitation and from the other side of the line a second male voice spoke before Mark responded. "I may or may not be sitting in a police station right now" He answered vaguely.

"Mark!"

"Well I didn't *mean* to get arrested, did I?" Mark retorted defensively. "How was I supposed to know that there was going to be a patrol driving past right when Kit and I…"

"Wait" Alice interrupted "*Kit and I*. Oh, Mark what have you done?" She moaned, closing her eyes in despair.

"Well don't worry they stopped us before I managed to get a good hit in"

"You were fighting!?" Alice cried out her eyes snapping back open in shock "*With Kit*!?"

"I wasn't *looking* for a fight" Mark admitted "I mean I was but I was never *really* going to hurt him too badly" Mark paused and hopelessly Alice leant back in her chair before Mark's voice came from her phone speaker again, quieter this time. "Kit's a better fighter than I remember. He's been practicing since we last…" Mark stopped short, as if he had accidently said too much.

Alice pursed her lips in annoyance. He was keeping things from her again but she knew as well as he did, why he had phoned her. This time *he* needed *her* help and granted this was a tad bit more serious than a runaway key ring but still, she owed him this much.

Not for the first time that night Alice lifted her hand to rub her face wearily. "Where are you then?" She asked "I'll come and pick you up"

CHAPTER TWENTY-SIX

Mark

OFFICER Jude Law was one of the very few NYPD officers in any precinct further south of the West Village Mark had not yet met.

The young man was brusque and straight forward with a booming Bronx accent that filled any given room he happened to be in and a deep, raspy voice to match. He was a large man; broad shouldered and shirt straining to fit around his chest and arms but Mark had seen his type before. They pump iron in the gym and rep their own body weight on the bench press but not one of them was useful in a fight.

Deep down they were all push overs. Mark could see Jude standing on a pedestal half a year into his career, proudly holding an employee of the month award for helping a little old lady cross the street on his day off. Officer Law had still put on a curt front since Mark had been brought in, in the small hours of the morning, though. Even now, as he stood in the doorway of Marks holding cell he wore an expression of condemnation.

"Up you get then" He spoke, nodding his head towards the bland and sad looking hallway outside. Silently Mark complied, standing from the uncomfortable, lumpy cot fixed to the back wall of the small room before slowly moving past the large man and towards the front desk he had been checked in at earlier.

Next to the counter, Alice stood, wearing the same grey NYU sweatshirt and dark wash jeans she was wearing the day they had met and a very unamused looking face. "You're lucky they've decided not to charge you otherwise your girlfriend would be picking up a hefty check" Officer Law spoke as he stepped behind the tall desktop and started flicking through a pile of papers in a cheap plastic tray to his right.

Alice spoke before Mark could.

"I'm not his girlfriend" she replied shortly crossing her arms and glaring at the man beside her "And I most certainly *won't* being paying *anything* for him" Sheepishly Mark ducked his head and half-heartedly Officer Law attempted to hide the smile that had appeared across his lips before he slid a single sheet of paper towards Mark across the countertop. "Just a little bit of paperwork" He explained looking down again to locate a pen and slid that over to him also "Sign just there please and I'll go and get your stuff"

Mark nodded quietly, taking up the pen and clicking it as he scanned no more than the title of the printed piece of paper before lowering the point to the white sheet and carelessly scratching his name over the black line Officer Law had pointed out to him. When he was done, Mark dropped the pen on top of it and pushed his hands into his jeans pockets staring down at his feet as, tensely, he and Alice stood in silence. Until Alice broke the quietness to speak irritably.

"If you didn't get a good hit in Kit certainly did" She grumbled crossing her arms "You're a bloody *mess*" Mark remained silent unsure about what to say. This had been the first time he had *properly* had the chance to speak to Alice in over a week and now that he finally had the opportunity to make everything right he didn't have a clue what to do.

"Come here. Look at me" Alice spoke cupping his cheeks gently to turn his head towards her. Mark cringed. He had thought he would be met with a face like thunder, with undisclosed anger on full display but when Mark finally let his gaze fall on her own face, all that looked back was fear and concern. Alice lifted her hand to touch Mark's temple softly where there was a tiny almost invisible scar from his last fighting injury.

"It's only just healed" she whispered sadly, stroking the small blemish with her thumb "And you're already all bloodied again" Mark's brow furrowed. Perhaps anger would have been better. This reaction was more jarring, less familiar than the heat and asperity of anger. Right now, Alice looked like she was about to cry and it made Mark feel sick to the stomach as her eyes filled with shimmering tears.

Quietly she sniffled releasing Mark's head to turn back to the counter as Officer Law returned with a dark wash denim jacket similar to her jeans and a plastic zip-lock bag containing his keys, phone and wallet. "I'll have to patch you up again when I get you home" she said watching the second man place Mark's things on the counter and pull the sheet Mark had just signed from the surface.

"Ok, looks like everything is in order" Officer Law told them sliding the sheet into a second tray to his left and looking back up to them "You're free to go but mind you don't be getting into any more drunken fights anytime soon" he warned glancing down at the computer in front of him to click at it a few times as Mark gathered together his things and Alice began to move towards the doorway behind them leading to the small car park outside the station.

"Don't bother" Alice mumbled under her breath glaring at him as he hurried to catch up to her walking through the doorway "He doesn't even listen to people who *actually* care about him" Quickly Alice moved out into the cold night air, her breath exploding from her lips in a cloud of condensation as she wrapped her arms around herself moving straight towards her car on the other side of the dimly lit tarmac area. "Alice!" Mark called out as he hurried after her "Alice let me *explain!*"

"Explain *what,* Mark!" Alice shouted, turning suddenly with her fists clenched and face wet with tears finally sliding down her flushed, blotchy cheeks "Explain why I got a phone call at nearly one o'clock in the morning telling me that you're locked up at a police station with no one to come and pick you up but me!?" She suggested, angrily stomping back towards Mark and throwing her hands in the air in frustration "Or why you're *constantly* looking for new ways to sabotage yourself and *somehow* manage to drag *everyone* down with you!? Or why for some awful... sadistic... *cruel* reason you seem to find *pleasure* in inflicting pain in others?"

 Unexpectedly Alice shoved Mark roughly, making him stumble backwards with his eyes wide in surprise. "*Why,* Mark! *Why*!?" She sobbed, her crying nearing hysteria now as she continued her assault and Mark desperately lifted his arms to shield himself from her blows. "Why do you *insist* on *worrying* me and *scaring* me and *putting me through the wringer over* and *over* again!" Suddenly Alice pulled away shivering in the freezing winter temperature with nothing more than her sweatshirt to keep her warm and uncontrollable tears streaming down her face.

 She might have said something else as well, if it weren't for the interruption that came from an obscure corner of the open area. The only place for a hundred metre radius untouched by the bright white streetlamps surrounding them.

 "Hi guys!" Jay exclaimed brightly stumbling out of the darkness to join them in the light with a smirk on his face and a cigarette hanging haphazardly from his mouth "Having a lover's tiff are we?" he spoke, his words slightly muffled as he spoke through the now nearly burnt out cigarette butt between his lips. "Fuck off, Jay" Mark retorted, straightening up now that he was no longer under attack "Haven't you done enough damage for one lifetime?"

Jay lifted his arms in surrender, an innocent look on his face. "What have *I* done?" he asked insolently "I don't know if you realised, Marky but *I'm* not the one who almost ended up having to spend the night in a cell" He pointed out "If it wasn't for your little girlfriend here…"

"For the *last bloody time* I'm *not* his *bloody* girlfriend!" Alice snapped, her fists clenched at her sides so hard her knuckles were beginning to turn white. Jay turned to her in surprise before his smirk returned and boldly he reached to wrap an arm around her waist. "Does that mean I'm in with a…"

"Touch her and I'll make you wish you were dead" Mark interrupted as he batted Jay's arm away and moved to put himself between him and Alice. Jay barely blinked, though, and didn't hesitate to move so that he was so close to Mark their noses were almost touching. "You would know all about that wouldn't you, Mark. I mean, after Jacob…"

"I wasn't behind the wheel that night!" Mark exploded snatching Jay's collar and shaking the older man roughly. Behind him he could hear Alice whimper in shock and quickly her hands were grappling at his shoulders, trying to pull the pair apart. "Neither was Eli" Mark growled, ignoring Alice's desperate begging to get him to stop "I'm as guilty as he is of killing Jacob" Jay was laughing now, almost as hysterically as Alice was crying. "Yeah, by association" He countered.

"How dare you!" Mark roared shaking Jay so hard his head swung back a forth on his neck like a broken bobble head. "Mark, stop!" Alice cried out desperately, now at his side in a flurry of panicked movement. "After everything you've done!" Mark yelled lifting his arm with his fist clenched high above his head when suddenly Alice's own arms were wrapped around it, tightly, the small girl virtually hanging off his bicep to prevent him following through with the action. "Jesus *fucking* Christ Mark! You *just* got out!" Alice sobbed.

Mark looked down at her in surprise, as if he had suddenly been broken from a trance and brought back to reality with a jolt. Slowly his arm was dragged down by Alice's bodyweight but she held on tightly, refusing to let go as Mark continued to keep a firm hold on Jays collar with his other hand. "Don't do it again, Mark. *Please, please* don't do it again" she begged him quietly, her breath coming in deep, struggled gasps as she fought to regain her composure.

If it were possible, Alice's skin might have paled even further from white to almost translucent out of fear but all Mark could see, as he looked down at her, were blotchy patches of red and pink on her otherwise ghostly complexion.

She continued to cry, helplessly and fearfully and it was that, combined with the raw, red rim that had appeared around Alice's eyes, that made Mark release Jay's collar and shove him away roughly. As much as he wanted to make Jay suffer like he and Eli had suffered, he knew Alice was right. He was outside a police station and not *just* a police station. A police station he had been released from minutes ago. Even the opportunity to hurt Jay wasn't worth the risk of being caught fighting twice in one night, least of all where he was stood currently.

Mark turned on his heel, dragging along Alice, who still clutched his arm, behind him as he stormed away from his so called friend and Jay shouted insults at them from where he stood in the centre of the car park. There was only one rule Mark had in his life, and it was the reason he was being picked up from this station and Kit wasn't.

You never throw the first punch.

CHAPTER TWENTY-SEVEN

Alice

 MARK'S apartment was deathly quiet as Alice worked silently to clean Mark's face and knuckles of the new blood and cuts he had been covered in.

 At some point during their journey from the station to Mark's small flat Alice had run out of tears to shed and had managed to compose herself enough to buy a pack of antiseptic wipes and plasters in a nearby pharmacy before finishing their journey in the same tense quietness they sat in now.

 It hadn't escaped Alice's attention that Mark had older injuries that had appeared since the last time she had seen him but, deliberately, she remained quiet, refusing to speak about it anymore. She didn't even want to know how many fights Mark had got himself into since their argument. She knew she wouldn't like it.

For more than thirty minutes, they had been sat in Mark's tiny kitchen area until, finally, the silence was broken by Mark.

"He was my best friend"

Alice froze midway through discarding the unwanted packaging left by the used plasters. "Jacob" Mark clarified "He was my best friend. Right from when I first moved here with Dad" Slowly Alice turned to face him, almost as if she was expecting him to panic and suddenly fall quiet again if she moved too quickly. "We went through everything together" Mark smiled sadly "Middle school, high school. He even got into the same course as me at NYU"

"You were at NYU?" Alice asked leaning back against the worktop behind her. Mark had never mentioned it before. Not when she had worn her college sweater or when he had seen her schoolwork. Not once.

Mark nodded looking down at his hands in his lap "Mhm" He hummed as if it were something to be ashamed of. "We were studying Mechanical Engineering and Mechatronics" Mark chuckled but not as if he found funny. It was more of a sad, woeful chuckle like he was trying to hide how he was truly feeling. "I was going to build robots. Invent things. Like my Dad" Mark cleared his throat turning away from Alice as tears glistened in his eyes "B-before he got ill"

Alice might have gone to him. Tried to offer some reassurance but something about it didn't feel right in this situation. Something told her this was something Mark needed to do by himself. All in one go.

"I tried to stay" Mark told her his voice becoming stronger as he sniffed and blinked away the tears building in his eyes "I worked two part times to pay his medical bills and my tuition fees but there was no point. I was falling behind and I was close to failing my first year" Mark paused "I dropped out" He admitted "And Jacob stayed on, met these two guys, Sam and Robin. Said they could help me pay my debts then I met Eli, Jay and his brother, Hunter, through them. I thought it was a quick fix and told them I would pay them back somehow"

Alice could feel her heart beginning to sink. "And then I got dragged into one of their fights by accident" Mark hesitated "I was just in the wrong place at the wrong time. I didn't want to fight but I owed them one, I couldn't just turn my back when they were getting beaten to the ground after they had paid off my debts. So, I helped them but w-when I hit the guy. I-I…" Mark took a deep breath, like it was actually physically hurting him to tell Alice all this. "It was the first time I really felt like… I was *coping*. I didn't have to *think* anymore. The only thing I needed to focus on was *not* getting killed"

Finally Mark looked up at Alice, an almost pleading look on his face and Alice could tell he wanted to cry. That he wanted nothing more than to curl up into a ball and be a small boy again who didn't need to worry about the things real Mark needed to worry about.

Mark gulped. "I don't know when I started being like them" He confessed looking away again when tears finally started overflowing "But I *did*. I started fighting and I started drinking and breaking the rules and I know that that's why Jacob's dead"

"But I thought you said it was Jay's…"

"It is his fault" Mark interrupted swiping away his tears as quickly as he could but for every tear he swiped away another appeared "*He* killed Jacob but *I* gave him the opportunity" Alice frowned in confusion. "That night, two years ago" Mark explained "The night Jacob died. My dad and his cancer. It suddenly got worse. Much worse and I was here. On the rooftop with Jay and the others, drinking till we couldn't see straight when I got the call from the hospital. I was too off my face to drive though" Mark squeezed his eyes shut, a pained expression on his face "So, Jake said he would drop me off and then come back but Jay and the others decided they wanted to go to The Black Tiger Club you know the one where I…"

"Almost got killed" Alice finished crossing her arms as she recalled the night. Mark nodded slowly looking down at his lap again, this time in shame. "Anyway" Mark went on "They said they would follow in another car and go on after they had dropped me off at the hospital but after they left me at the entrance, their car swerved in the lane next to Jacob's" Mark's fists clenched and his jaw tensed "He got pushed off the road and straight into a building" He let out finally, fresh new tears sliding down his face "And *Eli* got two years jail time and a four year ban on driving"

A moment passed as Alice processed the story she had just been told until something didn't add up. "*Eli* went to jail?" She questioned. Mark nodded his tears less sad and more angry now as his whole body looked like it itched to break something. "Eli went to jail because he took the fall for *Jay*" Mark was now so tense his hands were shaking and the veins in his neck stuck out "Jay was driving that night but Eli said it was him. It wasn't like he was going anywhere in life and he hadn't had as much to drink so why not? It was the dream for him. Two years where he didn't have to worry about paying rent or bills or buying food" Mark paused "Jay *killed* a man and got to walk away *scot free* and God knows I should have stopped there. I should have walked away and found other ways to get by but with Dad and Jacob gone I had no one left but them and it just got worse and worse and..." Mark trailed off gesturing to himself weakly "And here I am now"

Alice stood opposite him, frozen in stunned silence. All this time she had been waiting for him to open himself up to her just the tiniest bit and right then he had poured his heart out to her so fully she hardly knew what to do with all this new information she had been given. His story answered all the questions she had been asking since the very first time they had met. Why he was so cold. Why he was so fiercely independent. Why he was so set on sabotaging himself over and over again.

He had been alone since he had been Alice's age. At the most crucial part of life when you are released into the world and you need the guidance of a parent and the support of a friend. But poor Mark had been forced to do it all with neither. No wonder he found it so hard to pull away from Jay's group despite all they had done. He and his friends had become Mark's only family and the habits he had picked up from them, had become his only way of coping.

"Mark…" Alice began but before she could think of anything else to say Mark was standing, stumbling out of the kitchen area clumsily and towards the door at the back of the apartment leading to what Alice could only assume was his bedroom. "Wait. Mark. Where are you going?" The least he could do is offer her the chance to respond in the right way before he *decided* whatever she was *going* to do was the wrong way.

"To find a new t-shirt" Mark responded flatly not even turning back to her "This one's dirty" Alice looked down at the dark shadow of half dried blood on Mark's simple black t-shirt before hurrying towards him suddenly when he tripped over the small coffee table in the centre of the room. Quickly she grabbed his arm and guided him to sit down of the sofa beside them heavily.

"Why don't *I* go and get you a new shirt?" She suggested as she released Mark's arm and turned to move towards the doorway Mark had been heading to himself. Mark made a noise from behind her, as if he had begun to protest and then thought better of it when Alice had already entered the room. "Where do you keep them?" She called out the open bedroom door as she stood in the centre of the room, unsure on whether she should head for the wardrobe or the chest of drawers beside it.

"In the wardrobe" Mark called back making her move to the larger of the two cabinets quickly, kicking aside another dirty t-shirt to the side as she pulled the doors open and yank out the first shirt she could find when a flash of red from below her caught her eye. Curiously, Alice crouched down over the white t-shirt she had just kicked to the side and scooped it up with her free hand. "*Mark*!" She called, straightening up to walk out of the room and back to where Mark was still sitting in the living room. "You *still* haven't cleaned the last shirt you got all bloody?" Alice asked holding the garment up for him to see.

For a moment Mark looked panic stricken, as if he was student suddenly being caught smoking behind the bike shed but quickly he recovered when Alice shook her head light-heartedly and chuckled. "Honestly, Mark. *How* are you still alive?" Half-heartedly Mark laughed with her, watching as she moved towards him from his bedroom doorway and dropped the stained garment on the coffee table opposite him.

"Arms up" She instructed placing the clean shirt beside him on the sofa. "I think I can dress myself" Mark said starting to pull his dirty shirt from his body when Alice caught his wrists quickly and lifted them high above his head. "I'm sure you can" She agreed, pulling the shirt over his head herself, carefully "I just don't trust you not to make more of a mess and get blood all over your sofa that *I* am going have to clean up"

Hastily she bundled the shirt up into a ball before it could drip on the floor and bent down to gently mop up the left over blood on Marks back and shoulders with it. Thankfully, the blood hadn't dried too much and Alice was able to clean most of it away quickly until suddenly Alice was hit with a wave of bashfulness when she reached Mark's bare chest and Mark leant up to whisper in her ear in response.

"Touché"

Abruptly, Alice straightened up. "Touché, indeed" She mumbled, picking up the clean shirt beside them and dumping it in Mark's lap before she scooped up the other dirty shirt from the table and moved past him again. This time it was to his kitchen area, where she quickly located the old, battered washing machine tucked under the worktop and threw the shirts in unceremoniously.

"Of course you wouldn't have run out of these" she joked lifting an unopened box of washing machine pods as Mark quickly pulled on the shirt from his lap and looked up at her to see what she was speaking about. "Do you *ever* do your laundry?" she questioned. Mark lifted his hands as if in surrender "I do!" He defended, watching Alice pull the box open and throw a capsule in after the garments, rolling her eyes in disbelief.

"Sometimes" Mark added quietly, making Alice hum in agreement.

"I thought as much" She responded, pressing a few buttons on the machine before returning to Mark's position on the sofa. Slowly she lowered herself onto the sofa beside him bending her knee to rest it on the cushion so that she could face Mark fully. A moment passed as she took him in fully.

It was the first time Alice had properly realised the way all his features melded all together to create one uniquely striking human being. It was no secret that Mark took very little care of himself. Over all the time Alice had known Mark, she had seen bruises tarnishing Mark's skin so often that they had practically become a part of him not to mention she had very quickly deduced that his diet consisted mainly of sugary corner shop snacks and… well. Air. Despite the constant shadow of wounds covering him, though, and the seemingly permanent dark circles surrounding his eyes. Mark was still a confusingly beautiful man.

It made Alice want to hit him out of frustration.

And kiss him.

And tell him that, somehow, it would all be ok.

All at the same time.

"What am I going to do with you Mark?" She murmured lifting her hand to gently tidy his hair where it had been tousled by his shirt. "You can't keep doing this" Mark looked down at his lap again "One day you're going to get really hurt" She told him softly "And I won't be able to patch you up"

"I won't anymore" He blurted out suddenly, his brow furrowing. Alice froze with her arm half lowered. Something about his uncharacteristic willingness to change the way he had behaved for so long, with no repercussions, when all he ever did was ignore her, had caught her off guard.

"I thought it would be better if you could just move on and forget about me and that way you wouldn't get sucked into my world, me and Jay and Kit's world but I *can't* stay away from you. I can't *focus* on anything without you. I can't *think* straight. I can't… *live* without you a-and I don't know what for but I *need* you." Mark paused running his fingers through his messy, unkempt hair undoing Alice's attempts to tidy it. "I need you but I don't want you to worry" He explained, quieter now "I *never* want you to cry like you did earlier. *Ever* again" He added, shaking his head as if he could detach the memory from his mind completely. "And about what I said the other day…"

Alice didn't let him finish. She had decided what she wanted to do and, just like he had, the night Alice had last picked him up after a fight, she pressed her lips to his in an impulsive, spontaneous act of bravery. Immediately Mark fell silent and tensed up in shock and for an awful moment, Alice thought he might push her away, like he always did. She was surprised, though, when Mark didn't push her away or pull away himself and instead he slowly let the kiss to intensify.

He leant forwards to deepen the kiss. He pressed his stomach flat against hers. Alice followed his lead when he took charge of the kiss and lay back against the cushions on Mark's sofa. It wasn't like their first kiss. During their first kiss Alice could feel Mark's body heat radiate through her own anatomy even through both sets of their clothes but this time Alice and Mark were both still cold from the freezing night air they had come in from. Despite this, though, their kiss was warmer. Less lustful and more loving as they pulled away slowly now, tangled in a messy pile of cushions and entwined arms and legs.

A moment of silence passed as they lay together, Alice pressed to the back of the sofa behind her and encapsulated in Mark's embrace as he lay opposite. Eventually he moved to rest his chin on the top of her head so that her face was buried in the fabric of his new, clean shirt. Despite it being fresh out of the wardrobe, it still had that distinct musky smell of cinnamon-y, winter fire smoke and evergreen trees that made it his. Alice welcomed the comforting smell. Until Mark spoke quietly, almost a whisper.

"Don't leave me again" He murmured, tracing soft circles against her shoulder blade with his fingertips. Alice remained still, thinking about what to say before Mark spoke again, sounding more sure than before. "I won't leave you again"

CHAPTER TWENTY-EIGHT

Mark

THE first thing Mark realised when he woke up was the fresh smell of outside air in his apartment. It was lighter than the much denser, dust heavy air that normally circulated around his stuffy apartment but rarely entered the enclosed space.

The second thing Mark noticed was another unfamiliar smell of cooking, making him open his eyes slowly to stare up at the ceiling above him. Quickly he closed his eyes again when bright light bounced off the white surface and made his eyes hurt. Mark turned his head and opened his eyes again and this time his eyes focused on the raw brick wall opposite his sofa, it's bricks now more of a dark orangey than a rusty red now that it was bathed in sunlight.

"You're awake" A voice came from above him.

Groggily Mark sat up and twisted from where he was now sat across the sofa he had fallen asleep on the night before to see Alice stood in front of his small kitchen's cooker. Kindly she smiled down at him as Mark let his legs fall off the side of the furnishing heavily and gradually his mind began to clear bringing him back to the real world fully once the remnants of sleep had finally left him. Quietly he let out a sigh as he stretched out his arms, as if it would bring some life into the lax muscles controlling them.

"W-what time is it?" He mumbled searching his walls for the clock he knew hung somewhere. He still wasn't quite aware of his surroundings yet. His bearings had been lost in his sleep and it felt like he was relearning each object in his flat and its position as he still squinted in the bright light. "Quarter past ten" Alice responded looking down to flip over the three rashers of bacon she was frying in the pan in front of her "You must have slept well. You didn't even make a noise when I got back with all this food" she told him and watching him when Mark pulled himself to his feet and stumbled in the vague direction of the kitchen worktop Alice was cooking behind.

On it was a large paper bag with bread, milk, eggs and various other essential groceries beside two white plates with a slice of toast and a fried egg on it each. Mark frowned as he watched Alice turn away from the cooker with a second pan in her hand. He had slept well but Mark couldn't even remember the last time he had slept properly *at all* leave alone slept *well*.

Alice, however, remained unaware as she finished her cooking and pushed one of the plates across the work top to Mark with a knife and fork. "Eat" She encouraged him pulling a carton of smooth orange juice from the paper bag to her right "I'm guessing you haven't had anything for about three days like usual" Alice added under her breath as she poured him a glass and slid it across the surface to him also.

Mark resisted the urge to correct her and tell her that it had actually only been a day and a half since he had last had a full meal and instead took the glass gratefully to swallow it almost in one go when the liquid touched his parched tongue. Alice smiled smugly and as if on cue Mark's stomach growled loudly only causing Alice to raise an eyebrow as if to say *'I told you so'*

"You didn't have to do this" He told her quietly picking up his knife and fork and cutting off a piece of toast to lift up to his mouth. Alice nodded slowly, looking down at her own plate of food as she ate opposite him. "No" she drew out swallowing a smaller gulp of juice than Mark's "But I wanted to" She continued "And you need food but *you* weren't about to fill up your kitchen were you?" Mark stopped chewing for a second, taken by surprise before he nodded as well. "I guess not" He answered, pulling a stool to his left towards him so he could sit down and take another bite of his food.

"Thank you" He said quietly pushing the mushrooms on his plate to one side so he could attack the two rashers Alice had served him with his cutlery when he realised how hungry he really was. "You don't need to thank me for cooking you food" Alice responded chuckling "It's a basic…"

"No, I mean for last night" Mark interrupted. Both of them stopped eating. Hesitantly Mark lifted his head to watch Alice as she chewed slowly, thoughtfully almost. "For giving me a second chance" He explained.

Alice remained quiet, a ruminative look in her eye. "Am I going to regret it?" She asked, placing her fork down. Mark pursed his lips. "Probably" He answered truthfully. The thought of when that time came made him cringe alone and for a second Mark thought Alice might get angry again. Or upset.

Or both.

She did neither though. She let a moment pass. Then she looked down. Then she smiled. Softly. A sort of half smile, an almost relieved smile. "You know..." Alice paused, as if considering whether or not to finish what she was saying until she shook her head, as if shaking away any doubts she might have had "I don't think I will" Mark tensed his brows furrowing in confusion as he watched Alice pick up her fork once again. "If there's one thing I've learnt from you, Mark. It's that can't just wait for everything to fall into your lap" Alice looked back up at him her fork half raised with a bite sized piece of toast on it "Sometimes you need to be more forceful and take whatever it is you want" She went on smiling wider "And I *really* wanted you, Mark"

Mark smiled himself. It was too late to do anything about it now. The fall had begun and the crash would come but he could at least let Alice enjoy it while it lasted. "I wanted you too" Mark confessed "I just didn't realise it until too late"

CHAPTER TWENTY-NINE

Alice

AFTER their conversation that morning neither Alice nor Mark had much of an appetite and most of their breakfast remained untouched on their plates. It had been discarded to the bin by Alice soon after going stone cold sitting beside the sink for hours before Mark had dragged her away from the small area back to the sofa and on top of him, the way they had stayed for the majority of that day so far.

It wasn't until well past lunchtime, that Alice realised how hungry she had become despite doing nothing but kay with Mark since eating the few morsels of the breakfast she had cooked and

Mark himself, still hadn't eaten a full meal since she had picked him up from the police station last night. At least.

"We should go and get food" Alice spoke quietly tracing circles on his stomach like he had on her back the last time they had lain together on his sofa. This time, they were cuddled together much closer in attempt to block the cold draft coming in through the open window above them.

Half an hour ago Alice had tried to move to close the opening but she had only been able to lift her head from Mark's chest for a second before Mark tightened his arms around her. "Don't move" He had whispered against her hair as he gently guided her head back to his chest. "I'll keep you warm" He had reassured her and like then, when Alice broke the comfortable, serene silence that had fallen over them, Mark's embrace intensified as Alice moved to look up at him.

"I'm not hungry" He replied "I don't want to go get food" Alice chuckled as Mark moved his arm to stroke her hair gently, still holding her close with his other. "What *do* you want to do?" Alice answered turning over slightly so that her upper body rested on Mark's and she could rest her chin on her forearm to watch his face closely "We can't just stay here all day" Mark scoffed sliding one of his legs underneath Alice's so that she was now

lain across him fully. "We can" He disagreed
confidently "I do that all the time"

 Alice rolled her eyes. "Mark, we need to eat" She
countered, smiling in amusement. "But I want to
stay like this" He responded quietly "I like it like
this" This time Alice sat up fully. "I like it too"
She agreed wriggling out of Mark's grasp to stand
up "But I'm also hungry" she added. Suddenly she
yelped when Mark wrapped his arms around her
waist still not allowing her to move far from him.
"Come on" she laughed "We'll go to the coffee
shop and get a panini or something, yeah?"

 Mark released Alice from his tight embrace to fall
to the ground dramatically his legs still propped
up on the sofa but his head and torso now on
ground below Alice as he looked up at her with a
forlorn expression on his face before huffing and
scrambling to his feet also like an overexcited
puppy.

 Alice rolled her eyes. It was as if a switch had
been flicked inside of him. Last night he had been
angry, then sad, then angry again and today...
Today he was *this*. He was wrapping her in his
jacket before they walked out into the frosty late
November air because she had left her apartment
last night with nothing more than a sweater on. He
was smiles and jokes as they walked to his black
Corsa after he had insisted he drive. And he was
sliding his hand into hers once he had rounded the

front of the car to the pavement Alice had climbed out onto, squeezing it gently as they headed towards the glass door of "their" coffeeshop, together.

CHAPTER THIRTY

Mark

THE shop was quiet when they entered, as normal. Unusually though, to their right as they entered, a small step ladder was propped up against the wall with the shops normal barista balancing precariously at the top as he struggled to pin an unnaturally bushy garland around the doorframe they had just walked through.

"Hi!" He exclaimed dropping the garland when he realised the two people below him "Hi, I'm sorry" He apologised scrambling down the step ladder to join them on solid ground and straightening out his clothes quickly "Just... decorating... you know?" He explained breathlessly as he hurried to move to stand behind the counter at the far right of the room. Alice nodded, smiling herself as Mark tried to keep in involuntary laughter and Alice began to wander towards the food counter further right.

Quickly Mark forgot his amusement and tightened his grip on her hand.

Last night had been the first night Mark had slept. Properly slept. And the only thing that was different last night was the fact that Alice had been with him. Curled up and pressed against his side for the entire night. He could still feel the phantom of her tiny body against his ribcage. It was comforting and he was hungry for any other physical contact he could get from her. God forbid it was taken from him so soon, however temporary it may be.

Immediately Alice turned back to him a frown on her face as Mark attempted to pull her back to him, closer. A moment passed before Alice's frown disappeared and was replaced with a small smile, this time reassuring as, gently, she squeezed his hand back and hesitantly Mark released her hand so that she could continue on to the food and he, to the till as the barista tapped at it quickly "It's that time of the year again" The barista joked half-heartedly, pointing to an old looking stuffed Santa Claus decoration beside the register he was now stood behind.

Mark raised his eyebrows, lifting his head as if he were going to nod but stopped half way instead of bringing his chin back down fully and instead stopped just before he completed the nod to look down at the man. Uncomfortably the barista shifted before smiling welcomingly once again "What can I get you guys then?" He questioned tapping the till once again before looking to Mark expectantly.

Mark took a deep breath in through his nose as he looked up at the chalk board, considering what to order. "One black Americano and…" Mark paused glancing over at Alice as she pulled a second panini from the shelf she was stood in front of and turned to join Mark at the counter. "A honeycomb skinny latte" He ordered wrapping an arm around her waist as she placed the two paninis on the counter beside the till. His side tingled again as her body heat spread across his own body warming it from the cold air it had been exposed to just a few moments ago. Mark made a mental note to invest in a new jacket. Alice looked better in his than he did, the moment he put it on her he had decided that she was keeping it but it wasn't until now that he realised that he really did need a coat of some sort at least. "Of course," The barista answered tapping his order into the till "Is that eat in?"

This time Mark completed the nod he gave in response, pulling his wallet from his pocket with his free hand. "Oh no" Alice interjected fumbling through her pockets suddenly "I'll…" Mark raised an eyebrow as Alice's let her shoulders drop as if to say, *'I thought so.'* It didn't take Sherlock Holmes to work out she had been in such a rush last night she had completely forgotten to bring anything other than the clothes she was wearing and her car keys. Frankly, it was a wonder Alice had made it so far into her investigation when even *she* hadn't realised it until then.

"That will be seventeen dollars seventy, sir" The barista spoke politely oblivious to their interaction as he turned the card reader to the pair of them and Mark swiped his card over it smirking smugly. Satisfyingly the machine beeped to signal the transaction had been approved and Alice pursed her lips to hide the smile Mark knew was threatening to settle on her own face as the barista pulled the two paninis towards him from Mark and Alice's side of the counter. "Perfect" He said turning away from the counter to pull the two sandwiches from their packaging and place them in an old looking panini press beside the large coffee machine he moved onto soon after. "I'll bring your food and drinks over to you in a second if you want to go and find a table to sit at"

"Thank you" Alice replied gratefully moving away from Mark's side, much to his dismay and taking his hand once again to pull him towards an empty table beside the large window at the front of the shop. Suddenly Mark stiffened as Alice moved towards the large, exposing sheet of glass making Alice turn back to him for the second time since entering the shop. A moment passed as she looked at Mark in confusion before glancing back at the table she had been leading them to. Quickly Alice changed tack, taking a seat in a nearer table just beside them and tugging Mark down gently to sit down opposite her. "Is here ok?" She asked smiling softly as Mark allowed her to pull him into the only other seat at the small two person table, their hands still clasped together.

It was like a new medium of communication for them. For all the talking they used to do a thousand words seemed to be able to be replaced with just a single touch or the gentle squeeze of a hand, that Mark responded to Alice's question with now, prompting Alice to nod quietly before moving on as if she knew that this was neither the time nor the place to broach the subject of his strange opposition to windows.

"I was thinking I might visit Abigail's mother today" She told Mark releasing his hand to allow the barista, who had since warmed their food and made their drinks, place a large tray on the table in front of them and deposit their things to the wooden surface. Again Mark froze, his coffee cup half raised to his mouth this time. "Y-you were?" He responded. Slowly Alice nodded, watching Mark carefully as Mark lowered his cup back down to the table behind his plate of food. "I've been meaning to since Kit..."

Alice stopped short when Mark's jaw clenched looking worried. Mark forced himself to relax. Just because Kit had manged to involve himself it didn't mean everything was ruined yet. Mark still had time to patch things up. He could still somehow sew all the shards of information he might have fed her into something that *marginally* resembled the truth at least.

Alice took a deep breath before trying another way. "I didn't want to go by myself" she admitted quietly taking Mark by surprise. Mark had expected something more, invasive. Something more like a cunning way to make it seem mandatory like she had convinced him to leave the apartment this morning.

Mark looked away into a corner somewhere pursing his lips in quiet thought before grimacing as if he were about to do something he knew he would regret and Alice's face lit up with hope when he turned back to her and looked at her with an eyebrow raised for a moment. "Eat your food before it gets cold" Mark told her as he picked up his coffee once again.

Alice gulped, looking down at her lonely looking panini and obviously trying not to let her disappointment show. Mark watched her as he sipped his coffee carefully before he broke the quietness that had fallen over them. "How are we going to get any investigating done if you're running on empty?"

CHAPTER THIRTY-ONE

Alice

RUTGERS Street was a run down, desolate road in Lower Manhattan occupied mainly by red brick, high rise apartment buildings similar to the one Mark lived in currently, except with a much larger and *varied* collection of graffiti on their walls. It was different to the more busy, bustling Midtown Manhattan hub that Alice resided in. It was eerily quiet for a city street with a sombre, uneasy feeling in the air.

Alice shifted uncomfortably as she and Mark stood outside the door of Abigail's mother's apartment with a long line of labelled door bells to their left, each of the small metal circles staring back at her like eyes burning holes into her very being. All of a sudden Alice felt like an imposter. Was this really, right? To bring up something so raw and painful in a selfish quest to prove to herself and others she did have what it takes to be a journalist. Of course, if she finally got to the bottom of it all she would hand every bit of information she had gathered to the police but suddenly something felt so awry.

Truth be told, ever since Mark had rejected the idea of visiting Abigail's mother so conclusively the first time, Alice hadn't had the courage to do anything more invasive then revising everything she already knew without Mark there to catch her if it all went wrong, like he had been before their falling out.

For all his flaws and changeability, though, Mark had become a somewhat safety net for her, as if she were a tightrope walker balancing, dangerously high above him and Alice was skating on thin ice now. If the New York Times found out about her betrayal her job would be in danger and if the culprit realised someone was on his, or her, tail… Who knew what was on the line?

Her life possibly.

It was a dangerous game she had got herself and Mark mixed up in but she was in so deep now, she couldn't bear to pull away. There were too many unanswered questions. Too much excitement she

had never had before she met Mark and now…
Too much attachment.

Alice took a deep breath. This was necessary. She
needed this if she stood a chance at finding
anything else about her daughter's death and it's
link to Jethro Garcia's own unfortunate demise.
'One second' she told herself. *'One second of pure
mindless bravery'* She exhaled. And pressed the
doorbell to 23d Rutgers Street. Alice almost
flinched at the broken buzzing that it triggered and
a moment passed before a tinny female voice with
a heavy New Jersey accent came from the
intercom beside it.

"Hello?"

Alice leant forward suddenly unsure about what
to say. "Um. Hello?" She responded quickly she
turned to look at Mark behind her worriedly. Mark
shrugged looking just as lost as Alice felt. *'Is it
her?'* he mouthed. Alice turned back to the
intercom.

"I-is this Mrs Wilson?" Alice stammered. The
lady on the other side of the intercom hesitated
before there was a crackling and the voice replied
"This is *Miss* Wilson"

Alice's heart skipped a beat and desperately she
forced her racing mind to come up with some sort
of response. "I-I'm sorry we're looking for the
mother of a girl called A-Abigail Wilson" She

responded. Again the woman on the other end of the line hesitated, this time for so long Alice thought she might have left them altogether before the intercom crackled again.

"Come in" The voice said before the door in front of them buzzed even louder than the doorbell and Mark stepped forwards to pull it open quickly before the window of opportunity closed. Silently he signed for Alice to go in first and wordlessly she complied, nodding in thanks as she entered the small, bland entrance hall and began her ascent up the rickety, old looking staircase directly opposite them.

The dilapidated steps twisted around the area of the stairway dizzyingly as they climbed further and further up until the pair reached the second floor above them where a middle aged lady wearing thick black eyeliner and a low neckline black tank top to match stood half in, half out a propped open doorway.

She was a petite but angular looking lady with her collar bones protruding through her orangey fake tanned skin and a stern but weary expression on her face as she eyed the two young adults moving into the hallway to stand opposite her.

"Are you Journalists?" She asked frankly, making Alice's eyes widen in shock. It took Alice by surprise how much heavier her New Jersey accent was without the interference of the crackly intercom to disguise it. Even after she was able to process the new dialect, though, it still took a moment for Alice to fully process the question she had been asked before realising the poor woman must have been inundated with visits and questions from various newspapers and magazines recently. Each more anxious for an exclusive than the last. Admitting that she was, in fact, another would almost undoubtedly result in the woman's front door being shut in their faces and frantically Alice tried to find a way of answering her question without scuppering her chances of getting her questions answered.

Alice stood there, opening and closing her mouth like a fish out of water until Mark stepped forward from beside her unexpectedly. "Um. No." He spoke offering his hand to the woman politely "I'm not a journalist. I…" He paused as the woman left his hand hanging in the air an expression halfway between thought and concern on his face "I knew your daughter" He explained carefully taking another tentative step forward "Me and my girlfriend just wanted to come to check if you were ok"

Suspiciously the woman eyed Mark and Alice was grateful that she was too distracted to realise the sharp breath Mark's words had caused her to take in. So it was official. He had said it himself and not *just* to her but to someone else too. He was practically announcing her unavailability to anyone within earshot. Alice smiled kindly at the woman when she turned to her also, forcing herself to not smile too widely.

Abigail's mother relaxed slightly letting the door behind her swing open fully so she could lean out of the doorway further and take Mark's hand cautiously. "Y-you knew Abigail?" She spoke quietly her expression softening to one of sadness as she shook Mark's hand. Alice lifted her hand to rub the back of her neck uncomfortably while, beside her, Mark nodded slowly. She always knew talking to a mother about her murdered daughter was never going to be pleasant but this level of uneasiness was even worse than any situation Alice could have imagined.

"Me and my friends used to go to her club" Mark answered quietly "Until…" he trailed off as he and Abigail's mother released each other's hands. This time it was the fragile looking woman's turn to nod looking down sadly. A heavy silence fell over the group before Abigail's mother stepped to the side suddenly. "W-why don't you two come in for a bit" She offered more kind now "I'll get you a cup of coffee or something"

Alice hesitated, taking half a step forwards and as if sensing her vacillation the woman smiled warmly and gestured into the apartment with her right arm as if to say, *'it's fine'* It was Mark who entered first this time, however, leading the way for Alice to follow suit.

Abigail's name wasn't mentioned again until all three of them were sat around a small kitchen table, each holding a watery cup of coffee in both hands. Quietly they sat there until Mark caught Alice's eye and nodded in the direction of Abigail's mother who was stirring her fifth spoonful of sugar into her own coffee absent-mindedly. Quickly Alice turned back to Mark her brows furrowed in worry.

All of a sudden Alice felt completely out of her depth. Like she had finally taken this pretending game too far and she had found herself in the very predicament she had guessed she would. She had questions yes. But they were big questions. Questions Abigail's mother didn't know the answers to alone. She needed to put more thought into what she wanted to gain from this visit. She should have planned more, thought ahead.

She was close to giving up then, standing up and excusing her and Mark until a photo frame above the table caught her eye and instantly Alice took the prompt, leaning forwards to break the silence as gently as she could.

"M-Miss Wilson?" she stammered. Quickly "Miss Wilson" looked up from her mug looking taken aback before her shoulders relaxed and she chuckled quietly "Please" She replied, "Call me

Mel" Alice paused before nodding and correcting herself warily "Mel" She glanced over at the other woman. Nothing. "I-is this Abigail's father?" she asked pointing to the photo frame hanging on the wall above them haphazardly.

Mel followed Alice's finger to look up at the photo herself. She scoffed. "That's him" Mel answered suddenly looking less upset and more agitated "But that's all he was" She added pushing her coffee cup to the side so she could lean her forearms on the wooden surface between them. "Took off as soon as he knew Abi was on her way. I thought she should at least know her father's face, though, so I put that up when she turned three" Mel paused picking at the dark, already chipped nail polish on her long nails before standing to pull the frame from the wall. She moved across the small kitchen to where a battered metal bin was stood beside the worktop end. "I guess it doesn't really need to stay up now does it?"

Alice flinched as the sound of glass shattering came from the opening of the bin Mel had just thrown the decoration into before scowling down at it for a moment until Mark spoke up. "Do you have any idea how it happened?" He questioned, his own mug abandoned to the side of the table also. Alice turned to Mark suddenly, in shock that he could ask such an upsetting question so outright. To her surprise, though, Mel seemed completely unfazed as she shook her head and returned to her seat slowly. "Only that it didn't seem planned" She responded "They wouldn't let me see any of the photos but apparently it was messy, you know? And she was… left. Out in the open, like the person panicked and just, ran off"

Mark bit his lip looking nervous, as if he had suddenly realised what he had done and wasn't sure what to do next. Alice felt the same way. Taken aback at how in her stride Mel had taken the question. Better than Alice's question on Abigail's father almost but Alice hadn't missed the sadness in her eyes. She was a Mark type. She didn't let on.

"And there was nothing that led up to it?" Alice spoke up taking the opportunity to stay on the subject "No strange behaviour? Had she mentioned any problems at work or with her friends?" Mel began to shake her head again when she stopped suddenly, an expression of realisation on her heavily made up face. "Well, there was this one thing" She started leaning forwards over the table as if she were about to tell them both a secret.

"There was a fight at the club she worked at. She told me about it maybe…" Mel thought for a second "A week before she died?" The way she spoke it made it sound more like a question and momentarily Mel turned to look at Mark and Alice as if they might know the answer. All she got in return however was an encouraging nod from Alice as she listened attentively. "There are fights all the time but this time one of her colleagues got caught up in it. She didn't see much but…"

Mel was caught off abruptly when Mark choked violently on the coffee he had just swallowed and slid back on his chair hastily to avoid the liquid getting on his clothes. "I'm – cough, cough – I'm so sorry" He apologised placing his now half empty mug on the mainly clear table as he stood up to look down at the rest of his coffee spilt on the floor "I-I'll clear it up. Thank you. No, no, don't worry" He reassured Mel who had handed him a roll of kitchen paper and was now moving to help him mop up the mess. "Carry on. It won't take long" Mark chuckled "It was just a little hot"

Alice rolled her eyes, remembering the coffee Mark had spilt in her own apartment as she turned back to Mel, who was returning to her seat once again. "Sorry about him" Alice apologised again "He's not very good at eating *or* drinking" she joked reaching to cup her own mug in her hands hoping to warm them slightly. She was disappointed, however, when she found that her coffee had cooled to a meagre lukewarmness and Alice's hands were left still cold.

CHAPTER THIRTY-TWO

Mark

MARK felt sick.

And he wasn't sure if it was because he had consumed the most food that he had in one day since Jacob and his father died or the borderline traumatic proceedings he had just experienced.

Or both.

It wasn't the violence. He could deal with the violence. Up until this very moment in his life, he *thrived* in the violence. The truth was, though, Mark had never seen the fallout of violence so up close. He had never witnessed the devastation it brought to those left behind.

It was frightening. He now knew how Alice felt all those times she had, had to pick him up and clean him up after a fight. He wanted to turn to her and beg for her forgiveness. He wanted to beg for forgiveness from *all* the people whose lives he had destroyed in the very same way.

Until he thought of the people who had destroyed *his* life in that very same way. He didn't see any of *them* begging for forgiveness for their actions but then again. Mark wasn't even sure if they *knew* of the repercussions of their actions. They weren't his problem anymore, though. They would get what was coming to them. The world had a funny way of bringing things back round to bite you. Mark's only concern now, was keeping out of all of it. Keeping Alice happy and enjoying the time he had left with her. Before *he* got was coming to *him*.

"I got her number!" Alice called waving a pocket sized notebook over her head as she ran to where he was stood at the bottom of the stairs leading to the entry way of the apartment building. "I told her it was so we could check up on her if we needed to" she added lowering the notebook once she finally reached Mark. Slowly, they began to walk down the street towards Mark's Corsa parked on the side of the road.

Mark hummed in response still trying to gather his thoughts when Alice stopped suddenly, falling behind him unexpectedly. Quickly Mark turned to look at her in confusion as Alice looked back at him with her brows furrowed in concern. Hesitantly, she lowered the notebook in her hands. "Are you ok, Mark?" she asked.

Mark took a moment to process Alice's question, blinking as if it might help the cogs in his mind turn faster before he quickly rearranged his face to form a smile. "Of course" He answered stretching his arm out to offer Alice his hand to take. "Why wouldn't I be?" he questioned in response. Alice shrugged before taking his hand hesitantly and lacing their fingers together "I don't know" She answered quietly pushing her notebook into her jean pocket awkwardly with only one arm free now. "You just seemed a little...off" Mark remained quite as they walked, trying to think of a response. "Like with the coffee" Alice prompted tentatively making Mark look down at her with an eyebrow raised.

"What about the coffee?" he replied.

"You spat it out and told us it was hot but mine had already gone cold" Alice explained looking as if she was starting to get annoyed. Mark realised he was going back again. To being closed off and defensive. So, quickly he attempted to make it right by laughing light heartedly to break the tension that had fallen over them. "I know you're kind of a detective now, Alice" Mark chuckled

"But not everything is as sinister as you think" Mark squeezed Alice's hand reassuringly still smiling but when Alice still looked at him dubiously Mark rolled his eyes humorously before leaning forwards to murmur in Alice's ear, as if he were afraid Mel might hear them even when they were well away from her home now. "I said it was hot because I didn't want to say it was disgusting" He confessed, smiling wider as he pulled back to see Alice's surprised expression.

A moment passed as Alice stood there with her mouth half open in surprise and for a second Mark couldn't decide if he thought she would agree with him or scold him but much to his relief soon after they began walking again Alice's lips curved upward to form a smile also. Mark's widened at seeing it, making Alice's grow further and his again. Then hers agai,n until Alice spoke her smile now so wide it looked as if it would be impossible for her to stop.

"Maybe we should have asked for tea"

"Oh my god" Mark answered shaking his head vigorously and squeezing his eyes shut "I'm not bothered about coffee but I don't think I can live with tea being ruined like that for the rest of my life" Alice gasped "You like tea too!?" She exclaimed. Mark looked at her incredulously. "You didn't know?" He questioned as if it was obvious when they reached his car and he dug into his pocket to retrieve his car keys. Alice raised her eye brows. "You drink two massive cups of black coffee in our coffee shop with me *every* evening faster than a cocaine addict inhales a line and you're telling me that you prefer *tea*" Alice summarised, an expression halfway between disbelief and astonishment on her face.

Mark chuckled, finally locating his car keys and pulling them from the folds of the garment. "*Yes*" He countered.

"But you're *American*!" Alice retorted jokingly making Mark drop her hand to push her away hard enough to show his displeasure at being lumped in with the rest of the population of the country they were in. "Oh sorry, sorry!" Alice spoke loudly moving back to Mark having stumbled sideways after Mark's push as Mark also spoke, beginning the very same sentence he had said the first time they had met.

"I'm not American" He started opening the passenger side door for Alice who stopped just before she climbed into the car to echo the next part in synchronisation.

"I'm *Taiwanese*"

"I know, I know" She admitted "I'm only joking" Alice told him as Mark leaned forwards, smirking mischievously. "I promise you I can do things no American *or* British man can, Alice Valetine"

Alice's face flushed bright red. Even more so than it was already from the cold and Mark tried, desperately, to hide how adorable he thought she looked with her rosy cheeks and wide, surprised looking eyes. "Maybe I'll show you sometime" Mark added enjoying the way Alice squirmed now that he had taken back control. Alice opened her mouth as if she were about to say something back but before she had the chance Mark pressed his lips to hers in a fleeting, stolen kiss that was over before it had the chance to begin.

Mark could hear Alice whine when he pulled away to move to the driver's side door and looked up at her to see her pouting. He paused chuckling. "Don't you want to get home?" He questioned "Didn't you say you wanted to make one of those boards with red ribbon?" Alice climbed in and closed the car door behind her. "I *have*" she replied matter-of-factly, crossing her arms as Mark started the car and put it into gear.

"Well" He said yanking the steering wheel abruptly to pull out between two cars moving past them quickly "I guess that means we have more time for something else then"

CHAPTER THIRTY-THREE

Alice

AS it turned out.

There wasn't much time for "other things"

Alice had spent the majority of the last two hours since they had arrived back at Alice's apartment sticking and pinning new, filled-to-the-brim post it notes to her "evidence wall" while Mark sat on the large sofa on the opposite side of Alice's apartment. He watched her patiently, silent until Alice turned to tell Mark she was going to change out of her now two day old clothes and Mark spoke for the first time since they had arrived when she returned a few minutes later.

"Is that my shirt?" He questioned smiling from where he was still sat on the soft, squashy sofa. Quickly Alice stopped at the coffee table in the centre of the living space they were now both in. She looked down at the outfit she had changed into consisting of comfortable drawstring shorts and a baggy white t-shirt she had grabbed carelessly from the top of the clean laundry pile near her bedroom doorway that, she realised now, looked more like a dress as it came past her shorts and almost halfway down her thigh. "O-oh" She stammered suddenly flushing bright red again. "I-it is. Sorry it was just the first thing I found. Let me go and…"

"No, no" Mark interrupted her, leaning over the table hastily to grip her wrist gently "No it's fine. You can wear it" he said reassuringly as, slowly, he pulled her round the table to guide her towards him and take her other hand in his free one. He smiled wider as he looked her up and down from his seated position. "You look better in it than I do" he added.

Alice smiled down at him in return only for her expression to change to one of bafflement as Mark gently pulled her towards him and closer again and when she couldn't get any closer that way, Mark dragged her down. Bemused, Alice allowed it, bending her knees to lower herself down slowly until Mark wrapped an arm around her waist abruptly and pulled her down to sit in his lap, simultaneously, pulling her legs up onto to sofa area beside him. "Keep it" He murmured, leaning back against the back of the sofa so that Alice could rest her head against his shoulder and involuntarily she took a deep breath in.

Alice wasn't quite sure at what point in the last two days that, his musky aromatic scent of crisp autumn air had become her single most favourite smell in the entire world. However, right here, right now, in this moment, she was ready to make a fragrance, mandatory for all men, identical to Mark's warm enveloping aroma, *purely* so that she would never have to go without it. Alice closed her eyes, savouring the closeness between them. Savouring every bit of Mark that touched her and every wave of warmth that passed through them.

"You're tired" Mark observed lifting his left hand to pull hair from her face tenderly and tuck it behind her ear. Alice kept her eyes closed. "Not tired" She answered quietly, making herself sound half asleep already despite the fact that she was actually telling the truth. Mark lifted his hand to stroke the hair he had just moved again.

"Not tired. Just…" Alice paused before finally forcing herself to open her eyes and look up at Mark. She couldn't bring herself to lift her head from his shoulder, though. "Just *weary*" Mark stroked her hair again. He didn't want her to either. So they stayed there, looking at one another with their faces centimetres apart before Alice spoke again.

"I'm just thinking"

"About what?"

Stroke.

Alice thought some more.

Stroke.

"Firstly, that I like this" She responded burying her face into his shirt once again. Mark chuckled. Stroke. "And secondly" She continued "I may not know *who* killed Abigail" Mark's hand froze just above Alice's head. "But at least I know *why*" Alice looked up again. "She *definitely* saw something she wasn't supposed to"

CHAPTER THIRTY-FOUR

Mark

THEY stayed like that for the rest of the day. Sometimes talking, sometimes just sitting and latterly, sleeping.

Alice had begun to drop off as soon as the sun began to sink behind the glass and metal trees that made the concrete jungle of New York and soon, Mark's hand ceased to move up and down to caress her hair like it had for the past hour. Not long after Mark's head lolled on the back of the sofa as his eyes began to shut tiredly until, suddenly, his eyes widened in surprise when the loud aggressive ringtone of Alice's phone filled the apartment with the incessant cacophony of noise.

 On top of him Alice jerked awake looking around in bemusement with her eyes still half closed. "Wha-?" She murmured sliding off Mark's lap to stumble into the coffee table making him reach for her instinctively until she rounded the furnishing safely "Where is my…" Alice trailed off when a yawn interrupted her as she wobbled to the dining table to start sliding papers around the surface in search of the ringing device. "Where *is* it?" She spoke as she continued to search in the dining area, now tossing papers to the ground in frustration.

 "Here!" Mark called starting when he realised the ringing was actually coming from the pocket of the jacket he had leant her earlier that day. Quickly he pushed his hand into the nearest fold in the fabric and slid his hand down until he found an opening to a pocket and the feeling of the sleek, slippery design of the phone reached his grip. Mark held it out to Alice as she rushed back to the sofa and snatched it from him before it could ring off.

 "H-hello?" She answered speaking before she even had a chance to get the device to her ear. Quickly she pulled it from her ear before pressing it back to the side of her face "Hell- oh! Kit! Hi!" Mark stiffened and quickly he sat up as Alice listened carefully to whatever he was saying on the other side of the line. "I don't know, Kit" Alice drew out biting her lip nervously "I'm with someone at the mo…" Immediately Mark was standing, pulling the phone from her grasp and pressing it to his own ear making Alice let out a cry of protest.

"What the hell are you playing at?" Mark snapped as Alice desperately tried to reclaim her phone. Mark turned away from her, however, making it impossible for Alice to reach her phone in his hand. "I thought I made clear to you about what I would do if you spoke to Alice again"

"Mark!" Kit's voice sounded through the speaker. His voice was bright, excited almost and it set Mark's teeth on edge "You know when I called my friend Alice I wasn't expecting to hear your voice. How strange" Mark's fist clenched. "Delete her number" He bit back lowly. Kit laughed condescendingly and Mark could hear Kit relay their conversation to someone else in the background before there was a shuffling and Kit's voice came through the speaker. "Listen, Mark" He spoke "We all know who's winning and who's losing here. I have stuff on you that can see you in jail for the rest of your life"

"We're all in the same boat you fucking idiot" Mark retorted. Alice let out a quiet gasp behind him. "I could put *you* behind bars just as easily as you could get me locked up"

 "You haven't got Jay on your side though" Kit responded darkly "Have you?" Mark's mouth shut quickly. A moment passed. "Put Alice on the phone Mark"

CHAPTER THIRTY-FIVE

Alice

THE only other time Alice had been this far into Lower East Manhattan had been the night she had taken Mark home after his fight last Friday but after Mark had reluctantly returned her phone to her Kit had insisted that she meet him at some car garage she had never heard of before. She was fully prepared to turn him down after all that had happened between him and Mark. There was no reason for her to add fuel to the fire and with Mark's help there was no reason for her to make matters worse between the two of them but when Kit had mentioned Jethro Garcia's name the temptation was too much to resist.

Alice couldn't afford to turn down any information about the deaths of Jethro or Abigail *or* the newest unnamed victim, now though. Not when she was so close to getting to the bottom of it all. The answer was there. It was within reaching distance. She just needed the last missing bits of information to fill the holes in her investigation. So despite the awful, crushing feeling of guilt it gave her and Mark's silent pleads for her to hang up, she agreed to meet him the following Monday.

"Just so that I can speak to him myself" She had reassured Mark once she had hung up the phone "I'd much rather spend the day with you, you know that but don't you think it would be better if I were to handle this whole Kit situation?" Eventually she had been able to convince him that it was for the best but even by the end of Sunday he still seemed forlorn. As if the world had just come crashing down. Like he was a child and his favourite teddy had just been ripped from his small hands.

Kit, however, seemed positively ecstatic once Alice had finally found herself at the address he had texted her the night before, sweeping her into a huge, suffocating bear hug at seeing her walking up the long, enclosed driveway leading to a battered, secluded warehouse backing onto a seemingly disused set of train tracks, "How is my number one journalist?" He questioned as he led her further up the gravel to a rickety old door with white paint peeling off the rotting wood.

"Tired" Alice replied light heartedly with a chuckle as she stepped through the doorway after Kit signed her to enter first with his free hand. "I'm not surprised if you *actually* do the work we're set in college *and* play detective at the same time" He responded closing the door behind him grinning "And let's not forget babysitting our friendly neighbourhood nutter Mr Marky" Kit added as he strode past Alice towards a second door where shrill, scratchy noises of machinery shrieks tumbled into the entrance way she and Kit were in each fighting to be heard over the others.

Quickly Alice opened her mouth to defend Mark but Kit barely left time for a breath before he went on turning suddenly to bow down with a flourish, dramatically. "But never fear!" He exclaimed "Your saviour is here!" Alice pursed her lips and quickly Kit looked up when he received nothing in response.

Kit straightened up.

"Ok, ok" He let out waving her through the second door into a large open warehouse space where a row of cars was parked at the far end and three or four bays across the length of it were occupied by burly overweight men in navy blue boiler suits, each working on repairing a car in someway or another as tinny twentieth century punk music played from a cheap speaker left on a desk in the top right corner of the warehouse.

"You remember I told you that Jethro guy was dealing drugs on the side of his bar work last week?" Kit reminded her as he ducked underneath a wire hanging low over the doorway they had just come through. Slowly Alice nodded, carefully moving under the same wire to follow Kit hesitantly as he guided her across the room towards the bay furthest from the large opening on the left of the room, the massive floor to ceiling doors shut tight to keep the cold out.

"Oi! Jay!" Kit called out already halfway across the room as Alice hurried to keep up with his long, gliding strides on her much smaller legs. Quickly the man leant over the vintage car in the furthest bay away looked up from whatever he was doing before dropping the large metal wrench beside a collection of other tools with a clatter to clap his hand against Kit's in greeting. "Kit" He spoke, his voice gruff and raspy as they bumped shoulders. "Jay" Kit huffed back as 'Jay' slapped his back hard and they pulled away so that Kit could turn on his heel to hold an arm out to Alice who stood just behind him timidly. "This is Alice the girl I was telling you about. Alice this is Jay" Kit introduced them smirking as he nudged Jay with his elbow and Jay wiped his dirty hands against a greasy rag he had just pulled from his pocket "Jay used to give Jethro the stuff he dealt with"

Alice clutched the hem of Mark's jacket she had yet to return and, frankly, had no intention to for as long as they remained together. There was something comforting in the scent of Mark encapsulated in the folds of the material, as if he were here with her in spirit even if he wasn't by her side in person and she most certainly needed all the confidence she could get as memories of Friday night in the parking area outside the police station sprung to the forefront of her mind.

Jay smiled sticking a hand out to her that, hesitantly, Alice took watching both men carefully. "We met before" He answered as he shook her hand before pulling his hand back to the rag in his other "What can I do for you Alice in Wonderland?" He asked chucking his rag on the ground also, once he was finished with it "You interested in Jethro are you?"

Alice opened her mouth to respond only to find her voice caught in her throat as both Jay and Kit looked at her expectantly. Alice coughed quietly. "I-I..." Alice paused biting her lip. "T-this was a mistake" She stammered spinning around quickly to hurry back towards the door she had just come through when Jay called out something that made her stop in her tracks. That made everything slow down and freeze.

Including her heart.

"Don't you want to know who killed him?"

EILIS O'SHEA

CHAPTER THIRTY-SIX

Mark

MARK knew as soon as Alice walked up onto the rooftop that she knew. Mark probably knew before she knew that she knew. Or would know anyway. Friday evening had been the end of the road for him and Saturday evening was when his luck had finally run out.

She was crying as she marched across the concrete towards him where he stood beside the small brick ledge at the edge of the rooftop, another bottle of rancid cheap beer in his hand as he leant against it and at least a crateful of empty ones sitting next to him.

Mark couldn't bear to move his gaze to her as she reached him. The sound of her ragged breaths and broken sobs were enough to make his own chest tighten and his own eyes sting as they stayed like that for at least a minute. Alice standing just behind him and Mark staring down at the busy street nearly one hundred feet below them.

He hated it when she cried.

He hated that it was always his fault. He hated that he was in her life. He *hated* that he couldn't find it in himself to save even the one person he *truly* loved in the world from himself.

Mark lifted the half empty bottle to his lips and took a gulp, grimacing at the disgusting stale taste it had. He fought back the urge to gag. He swallowed.

"You know then" He said, looking back up to stare at the building across the road from him. It was the same red brick as the one they were on now. Covered in the same dirty, distasteful graffiti as the one they were on now but far, far more deserted.

Alice sniffled.

"Tell me it's not true" She begged him.

Mark squeezed his eyes shut.

He wished he could. He wished with every part of his body that he could turn to her and explain every part of it away for her and hold her and tell her it would all be ok. But all he could do was turn his head slowly to look at her, a pained expression his face and Alice's face crumpled.

"Oh Mark" She whispered a whimper escaping her lips "How could you?" In that moment Mark felt like there was ten tonnes of bricks crushing him and ten grand worth of heavy machinery pulling him apart all at the same time and Mark didn't realise that tears of his own had begun to fall until one landed against his hand having dropped down from his jaw. And another. And another.

"I didn't mean to kill him" He choked his grip around his bottle tightening "I never should have been there in the first place" He added turning so that he could lean back against the ledge now "I had told Jay I wasn't going to help with his deals anymore Dad was gone and I had my job. I didn't need his money anymore but somehow he convinced me to do one more. Just to see the month through" Mark's hands were shaking now "I was only there in case there was any funny business but then someone said the wrong thing and Jay said the wrong thing back. Next thing I know, punches are being thrown and everything is blurry until he dropped down to the floor" Mark hesitated before he risked looking up at Alice who was watching him with a mixture of agony and horror on her face. "I didn't realise how hard I had hit him until he didn't get back up again. He was still alive when we left but the next day…" Mark paused to take a deep breath "It was all over the news that he was dead" Mark squeezed his bottle tighter to stop his hands from trembling "And that Abigail girl. She'd seen it all"

"So you killed her *too*?" Alice questioned her face blotchy and red but her skin so pale it was beginning to turn a sort of green colour. She looked as if she might be sick but Mark didn't dare make any move to reach for her.

"If *I* didn't then Jay would have" Mark mumbled looking down at his battered old converses as his head hung in shame "It would have been worse that way. He would have made her suffer"

"That doesn't mean *you* had to kill her!" Alice exclaimed "You could have gone to the police!"

"To get myself wacked behind bars because Jay fucked up just like Eli?" Mark retaliated "*I'm* the one who hit him, Alice! As far as the law is concerned *I'm* the one in the wrong and Jay will walk away with nothing more than a fine for *possession* of drugs because *guess what!?* No deal took place!"

Alice let out a small, frightened sound as Mark threw the bottle he was holding across the roof top and violently it shattered against the concrete ground behind her when, suddenly, it was like all the energy had been ripped out of him.

He slid down the brick wall behind him to sit on the same ground heavily.

"I hate myself" He murmured his head lolling on the bricks behind it aimlessly. "I hate myself for it but it was almost like I was getting back at him. Once…" Mark stopped, realising he had no idea how to express what he wanted to in words

"After…"

Nope. Wrong again.

"I was too far in" Mark confessed "I couldn't *stop* until I knew Jay would be behind bars before I was"

A moment passed, both their heavy breathing and small sobs being the only thing preventing silence, until slowly Alice slowly slid down the wall herself to sit beside him. "It's why you drink and you fight isn't it?" She whispered "So you get hurt"

Mark turned to her before nodding slowly. It had been a coping mechanism. Drink to forget, fight to punish himself.

"Sometimes" He answered.

"I mean, yes" He corrected himself "Usually. Except, with Erik" Alice frowned. "I was blind drunk" Mark explained "We'd just had that argument. About going to see her mother, Abigail's a-and I was angry and Erik was there and…" Mark stopped he couldn't use the same excuse again.

Not for *murder*.

"I-I didn't mean to" He repeated pathetically "I don't even know how the fight started, I just know how it ends"

Unexpectedly, Alice took his hand gently and for a second, just a second, Mark felt like everything had gone back to normal.

Until she spoke.

"Mark you need to go to the police" Mark pulled his hand away, lifting himself up from the ground again almost as if her very touch had burnt his hand. "You won't get sentenced to death, Mark" Alice insisted desperately scrambling up too "You're sorry for what you did and they're lenient with people who hand themselves in. If you would just…"

"No" Mark answered conclusively beginning to collect up the empty bottles on the ledge beside him "Not before Jay's behind bars" Desperately Alice grabbed his arm "You can tell them that too. You can tell them everything…"

"And watch when someone else goes to jail for him" Mark snapped pulling his arm out of her grasp roughly "*Again*" He added bitterly "I said no"

Alice's face hardened.

"You can't kill anyone else Mark"

"Of course I can't!" Mark exploded "I'm already at my wit's end! I *already* can't fucking live with myself!" Glass bottles went flying off the ledge as Mark threw his arm out in frustration and both he and Alice watched as they tumbled down to the street below and smashed to a thousand tiny pieces when they landed on the hard concrete.

Mark dropped the bottles he was holding.

"Mark…" Alice started watching as Mark turned to face the ledge and braced both his hands on the top of the wall ignoring her "Mark what are you do…"

Mark hoisted himself up.

"Mark stop!" Alice shouted struggling as she rushed to follow him up in a panic and throw her arms around him in a desperate attempt to keep them both on top of the ledge "This isn't the way to fix this!" Alice frantically tried to reason with him. Mark looked down at her incredulously.

"What do you mean *fix* this?" He answered almost laughing at how ridiculous it sounded.

How could you possibly fix something as broken as those shards of glass below them?

"I can't *fix* this" He said tears soaking through the collar of his sweatshirt "*You* can't fix this" Mark glanced down at the street below again. He turned in Alice's tight grip so they were facing each other now. Alice looked up at him the horror on her face earlier now replaced with terror.

"Alice"

Mark's voice was soft now, wobbly from his tears but tender as he lifted a hand to pull hair away from her wet face and tuck it behind her ear as another wave tears pricked his eyes. "I have nothing left to lose" He whispered making Alice let out a sob into his chest. "You have me!" She choked "You have me, Mark! Please!" She begged "Please don't do this!" Quickly she pulled her face away from his chest looking up at him again, this time pleadingly. "I-I love you, Mark"

Slowly, Mark shook his head his brows furrowing. "How can you love me after everything I've done?" He answered softly, gripping her shoulders gently as if the light squeeze might bring her to her senses but Alice only pulled him closer as she lifted her hands to cup his face gently. "What you've done isn't you, Mark" She answered "I *know* it isn't you" Alice paused, her eyes searching him anxiously for some sign, some *change* of some sort.

Mark lifted a hand to take hers in his. "I love you too" He echoed.

He squeezed it gently.

"So much"

He let go.

Alice's scream felt distant as the sensation of falling took over him. It wasn't frantic or panicked. It felt more like floating than anything else. It felt like everything was moving in slow motion instead of fast forward like it had for so long. For a few blissful moments Mark, possibly for the first time *ever*, felt peaceful.

Then he opened his eyes. And he saw Alice still leaning over the edge. Reaching for him but not growing smaller. She remained the same size, eyes wide with terror, mouth open in a silent scream and Mark realised why she was still no smaller than before.

Mark's heart jumped to his throat.

Everything was fast again.

She had fallen too.

ACKNOWLEDGMENTS

I can't believe I've just written a whole novel!

For as long as I can remember I have always wanted to write a full book and here I am today writing the acknowledgement part of my very own novel. I know full well that just like me almost no one will read this part but it still doesn't change the fact that this is probably the single most exciting thing I have ever written in my entire life and it's not even one of my stories!

Firstly I would like to thank my parents and two sisters who were in the thick of it all reading all my first drafts and listening to me moan on and on about what awful writers block I have. Thank you so much for putting up with me!

Secondly, I *have* to thank my best friend Lauren, who shares my love for books and writing and has supported me all the way through this journey. You've been there through the tough times when I've had nothing to write and all the good times right from the start. I hope we can continue to moan about our unrequited loves to fictional characters together for the rest of our lives.

This book wouldn't have been possible if it weren't for my amazing friend Sabaa whom I have spent many a media class with, fangirling over various male celebrities. Your support and constant optimism has been what's kept me going and kept me writing. Thank you.

I can't write a book without mentioning the three girls who quite literally dragged me through school kicking and screaming before we went our separate ways in Year Twelve. Ciara, Amalia and Katherine. Thank you for being the best friends when I needed you most and for continuing to be so, even over the distance between us all. May the C.A.K.E gang legacy live on well past our time.

A special thank you to all my English teachers who always encouraged me to follow my love of writing. Mrs Blake, Mrs Holloway, Miss Niland (I'm so sorry I can't remember your married name), Mrs Creswell, Miss Batka, Mrs McDonald and of course Mr Davies (even though you never actually taught me English) and to any other teacher who has supported me and nurtured my creative side including: Mrs Johnson, Mrs Hope, Mrs Meyer, Mrs Lee and in *particular* Mrs

Craven, the life and light of Coloma for me.

I would like to mention my primary school teachers to whom I shall be forever grateful to, in particular: Mr and Mrs Candia, Mr Woolmer, who founded my love of music, Mrs Watson, whom I still remember to this day for her witty remarks and her infectious hybrid of both optimism and pessimism (I'm *still* a bold girl), Mrs Easthope, Miss Gardner and all the staff who had the misfortune of teaching me at some dreadful point in their careers.

Also, Mrs Morrison, whom I distinctly remember read out loud one of my first ever stories about a Prince and Princess, to the entire school during an assembly. You were one of the few to witness the very beginning of this journey. A massive thank you to you.

And, finally, Mr Fagan-King. My Music teacher, IT teacher, Form Tutor, Head of Year and most importantly *hands down* the best PE teacher I've ever had. When you left our school I wrote you a letter in which I said I hope that one day I would make you as proud of me as I am of you. I hope that this is a moment where you look back on the younger Eilis O'Shea you used to teach and see how far I have grown and developed and achieved, mainly down to the lessons you taught me and the motivation you gave me to do as well as I possibly can. To you, I owe everything.

ABOUT THE AUTHOR

Eilis O'Shea is a dysfunctional, creative mind born in South East London in 2003. She spends most of her time reading romance novels and obsessing over an unhealthy amount of male celebrities because finding imaginary love is *much* easier than finding *real* love.

One day she hopes to move to Japan where there are endless amounts of cute coffeeshops she can sit and read in (and cute guys) but for now she currently resides mainly on social media at:

Twitter: @eilis_shea

Instagram: @eilis_shea

www.eilisoshea.com